Navy SEAL

TALKING DOLPHINS

Episode #4

Craig Marley (signature)

MELTDOWN

CRAIG MARLEY

ISBN-13: 978-1976460937
ISBN-10: 197646093X

Interior design by booknook.biz

CONTENTS

INTRODUCTION

Imagine a transcendent form of communication - thirty million years in the making - an infinite number of words, ideas, thoughts, and images melodiously transmitted above and below the water. Envision a brain containing terabytes of epochal information from a time long before humans existed. So it is with the dolphin - their ability to recite boundless streams of information in musical tones - and a mind eager to learn.

Lacking syntax and impossible to translate with the most powerful supercomputers, the language of the dolphin remains an enigma. After years of false hopes and failures, Doctor Greg Mason (SEAL) and his team of linguists discover the secret to communicating with these magnanimous animals. Rather than attempting to decipher their language -- *teach them ours.*

Under a presidential directive, Greg authored the United Nations Dolphin Equality Doctrine - a partnership between humans and dolphins - a global mandate to conserve and protect their mental, physical, and social well-being. And if these courageous, highly intelligent earthlings choose to work alongside humans as equal partners, we will provide the means for them to safely return to the wild whenever they wish.

Inherently peaceful, a few of these brave marine friends have joined humans as agents of virtue and justice in the fight against terrorists and criminals.

****

Upon graduation from BUD/S (Basic Underwater Demolition SEAL training), Lieutenant Greg Mason returned to the Naval College of Science and Technology, where he earned a Ph.D. in interspecies communication. He then joined DARPA (Defense Advanced Research Projects Agency) as principal investigator of a top-secret project, code-named *Songbook,* culminating in the creation of a revolutionary, computer-based language and translation system and the first generation of talking dolphins.

****

ISIS grew in notoriety through an aggressive social media and viral video strategy that glorified violence - jihad. They filmed the execution of many victims including beheading, hanging, drowning, burning alive, and shooting. When they captured a town or village, they institutionalized slavery, murder, and rape of the locals and commenced a reign of barbaric terror throughout their region of influence.

There are a number of forces that can explain the source of ISIS's strength. ISIS played on emotions by promoting a sense of victimhood and a means to use violence to regain respect. They preached a twisted interpretation of Islam that appealed to young Sunni Muslims, both men and women.

Racketeering, extortion, and taxation of the religious minorities provided ISIS with their initial financing. Later, as they gained power and influence, they smuggled crude oil into Turkey and sold it to the highest bidder. This generated tens of millions of dollars a month to fund their global acts of terrorism: jihad.

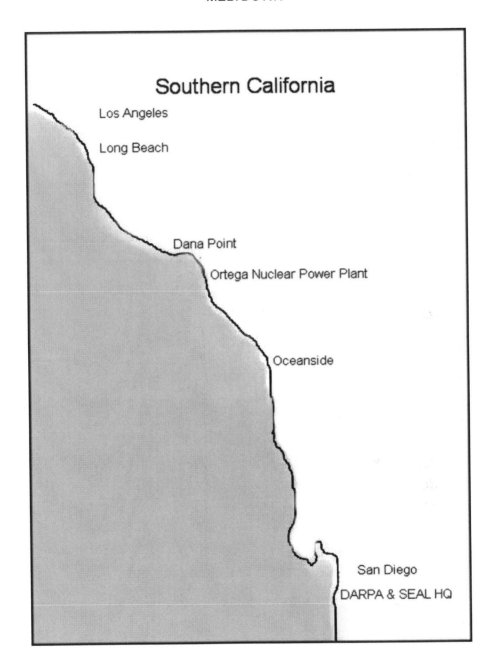

Southern California

Los Angeles

Long Beach

Dana Point

Ortega Nuclear Power Plant

Oceanside

San Diego

DARPA & SEAL HQ

WRATH OF FUKUSHIMA

On the last day I'll ever know
God be quick don't take me slow
Hammer the longest nails in straight
And let me pass your pearly gate
Hammer the thickest nails in deep
So I can face the endless sleep
Radiated planet abounds with death
All God's creatures out of breath
Radiated planet from winds afar
Slowly encircle our burning star
Radiated globe can no longer be
The mother of life wherever you flee
Feckless leaders scoffed at the blame
Unholy hearts played a global con game
Fat cats hide but bear no shame
Fat cats' doom comes just the same
The blistered and crippled no longer contend
The Mayan gospel was so penned

MELTDOWN

Dear wife and children gone long ago
All had succumbed to that invisible glow
So here I tremble heartbeats away
From meeting my maker this wintery day
On the last day I'll ever know
God be quick don't take me slow
Hammer the longest nails in straight
And let me enter your pearly gate
Hammer the thickest nails in deep
So I can face the endless sleep

OCEANSIDE

It was just past midnight on a moonless evening when he pushed the throttle forward and slowly powered the Grady-White past the Oceanside rock jetty and into the open sea. This would be a perfect night for the mission - the darkest night of the month.

As he headed up the coast he looked eastward, toward the lights from expensive oceanfront restaurants and multimillion-dollar beachfront mansions lining the shoreline and rolling hills.

His thoughts raced ahead to a blessed day in the future - a day he prayed for Allah to grant him and his followers - a day when not a single infidel would live in those gaudy palaces, drinking fine wine, overlooking *"their"* beach. It would be a glorious day for ISIS and Allah - the day the infidels simply disappeared.

He pushed the throttle to the limit, bringing the powerful twin outboard engines to a high-pitched rumble, sending a white rooster tail of sea spray high into the sky. The Grady-White bounced effortlessly across the four-foot swells, shooting a fan of foamy salt water off her bow as she kissed the crest of a wave. Flying fish, pectoral wings fully extended, flashed off the beam, sailing across the water a few inches above the surface, racing ahead to an unmarked destination.

Ahead, the lights from the Ortega nuclear power plant dominated the shoreline. Lit up like a Christmas tree and surrounded by a thirty-foot-high wall, it looked more like a massive beachfront prison than the largest nuclear power plant on the west coast of the United States, serving a population nearing thirty million people.

He knew plant security would likely recognize his intrusion shortly after he entered the restricted zone. But that was part of the plan: to learn just how quickly he would be apprehended, what assets would be deployed to thwart his progress, what the penalty would be if he was caught.

His mariner's map clearly showed the restricted area. A thick red line traced the perimeter, a rectangular box a mile wide extending a mile from the beach.

At each of the two seaward corners, warning buoys bobbed up and down, each one containing a flashing red light and a brightly lit sign reading RESTRICTED ZONE - DO NOT ENTER. Mounted high atop the steel mast, an infrared camera surveillance system fed its signal to a panel of monitors attended by some overweight, sleepy-eyed security guard with an addiction to glazed donuts and a propensity to grab a little shut-eye while on duty. Each buoy was home to one or more sea lions enjoying an evening of bobbing up and down while grooming their whiskers, head, and shoulders.

As he approached his destination, he put the engines in neutral and let the craft drift. Then, pulling two deep-sea fishing poles from their rod holders, he cast out his lures. This was a ritual procedure - something he had done every third or fourth night for the past month. It was his way of conducting a reconnaissance - gathering intelligence - assessing the strength and weakness of the infidels, to learn how much time he had after entering the restricted zone before he was discovered by the marine security patrol or apprehended by the US Coast Guard.

Under the pretense of night fishing, he put the engines into trolling mode and cruised past the first warning buoy into the restricted zone. As he crossed the invisible demarcation line a bright white light from the buoy lit up his vessel.

"Just as I suspected," he chuckled. "So now I'm on video." He looked at his watch and made mental note of his elapsed time as he continued with his plan, circling and making figure eights across the restricted zone while continuing to move closer to the Ortega power plant. He took a long pull on his bottle of water and seated himself in the captain's chair.

Looking up, he scanned the stars for Orion, the Big Dipper, and the North Star.

"They're still where they should be," he whispered. Thoughts of his mission wandered through his head. This was no ordinary mission. No way. This was the most important mission of his life. "Allahu Akbar," he blurted. He took another long pull on his water, looked at his watch, and turned to observe the huge containment domes of the Ortega nuclear power plant. "You have no idea what I have in store for you. It won't be long. You'll see."

He didn't need the money. His father had left him a small fortune from his Iraqi petroleum business. He didn't need the notoriety. He earned his brutal reputation while working for Saddam Hussein and the Ba'ath party movement, training young jihadists how to fight - how to die - how to achieve martyrdom and the seven blessings Allah promised in the afterlife. No, this was not about avarice or prestige, nor for the loss of an eye to an unseen sniper in the battle for Aleppo. No, it was not about any of that. He was motivated by pure ideological hate, driven by his belief in jihad and his pledge to Allah to eliminate infidels - the non-believers.

He hadn't always felt this way. It took many years. But over time, as his world molted and morphed into a raging war zone, he came to realize that the infidels orchestrated this everlasting, worldwide military conflict. These ultra-rich, sociopathic tycoons and power brokers were determined to usher in a new world order - and reap unimaginable profits. It was time to fight back.

As the ISIS movement galvanized, the theological leaders and militants declared a caliphate - a vast territory under the leadership of an Islamic steward considered the righteous successor to the prophet Muhammad and supreme leader of the entire Muslim community.

They preached a radicalized version of their theology and ideology and zealously administered the most brutal forms of Sharia law. They recruited, radicalized, financed, and equipped roving cells of jihadists, beheaders, and rapists, expanding their sphere of terror.

In order to brainwash their followers, ISIS clerics and mullahs took a lesson from the Nazi Propaganda Minister, Joseph Goebbels. He described it best when he said, "Make the lie big, make it simple, keep saying it, and eventually they will believe it."

Over time, the impressionable jihadists not only believed it - they embraced it.

Now, late in the first quarter of the twenty-first century, the smartphone became the prime-time provocateur - the Minister of Propaganda - dispenser of innumerable big lies.

This compact slice of electronics turned malleable minds away from traditional values and created a social media demigod - an unholy, highly addictive psychotropic monster. Within this toxic domain, glorifying winners was sinful. Everyone was equal in body, mind, and spirit; everyone received the same certificate of participation, in life and death.

Its addictive power hijacked the viewers and turned them into lemmings. It became their lord and master, kidnapping their individuality. Half the population of modern societies spent most of their waking hours mesmerized by selfies and the incessant drivel, blather, and banter about the latest tattoo designs, political correctness, who's gay, who's not, who's not sure. These were the hot topics - the soup du jour - turning formative hearts and minds into spineless zombies. They never left home without it.

But the real game changer came when millions of Muslim refugees flooded into Western Europe and North America including a preponderance of eighteen to thirty year old jihadists who nurtured and practiced ISIS principles and pledged their life to exterminate the infidels. Moreover, with fertility rate three times greater than that of the infidels, their numbers were growing exponentially.

"Allahu Akbar. Allah is great. Allah is righteous. Like snow-flakes and beached jellyfish, these infidels are destined to perish. They are non-believers. They must suffer and die!" he shouted across the water.

****

Off in the distance, he heard the security helicopter swooping in low from the south, and a bright searchlight scanned across the surface of the ocean. Moments later, he was illuminated by the blinding light. He glanced at his watch. "Thirty-seven minutes - five minutes slower than the last time."

"This is a restricted area - a red zone. Please leave immediately. This is a restricted area," boomed the voice from a loudspeaker.

Shielding his eyes from the intense beam of light, he waved at the pilot while yelling, "I'm just fishing!" He pointed to his fishing rods. "See? My lines are out. I'm not hurting anyone. Why do I have to leave?"

"This is a restricted area! You are violating the law. There's no fishing in this area. Leave immediately or we will call the Coast Guard. You may be ticketed or arrested. Your vessel may be impounded."

He waved and nodded as if he intended to leave. "Let's see how long I can stall them," he mumbled while smiling and waving goodbye to the pilot. He then slowly began to crank in his first fishing line."I might get a fucking ticket," he said facetiously.

The helicopter banked to port and headed south before he had retrieved his first lure.

"These guys are fucking idiots," he smirked.

The helicopter never returned - and neither did the US Coast Guard.

DOLPHIN TALK

"Good morning, gentlemen. Welcome to DARPA."

As the Director of Training, April Tanner looked over the determined faces of six SEAL senior enlisted men sitting before her.

"You've all completed the basic *Songbook* training program and have extensive hands-on experience with our dolphin partners in open water conditions. Today, we're going to introduce you to a wireless underwater version of the *Songbook* system with the computer worn on your wrist and the transceiver built into your full facemask. It is basically an underwater local area network. We call it DULAN - dolphin underwater local area network."

The SEALs looked at each other and uttered optimistic buzz words.

"This breakthrough technology will allow you to talk directly to the *Songbook* command and control station and to your dolphin and human dive buddies."

"Finally!" Chief Pace sighed. "We've been pushing for this for over a year. If it works, it will make a huge difference in the way we operate underwater."

"As you know, the biggest technical hurdle was miniaturizing the computer into a water and pressure-proof package and creating a suitable broadband transmission medium. We tried multiplexing, phase shifting and reverse polarization. We also had the challenge of encryption, firewall, and security. The coders finally worked it out. What we've got is five million lines of code - about the same as needed to fly one of our Reaper drones." April grinned and put on her "you won't be disappointed" face.

"How'd they manage to pull this off - what was the key to the breakthrough?" asked Chief Wagner.

"Sorry, Chief. If I told you, you'd soon be nullified." Everyone chuckled.

"So, gents, your wish has finally been granted."

April opened up the composite equipment case, removed the miniature waterproof computer and full facemask, and held them up for everyone to see.

"This is it gentlemen - DULAN - six ounces of high-speed talk-to-text, text-to-talk underwater communication system. The computer includes the LCD monitor, digital clock, decompression calculator, compass, touchpad keyboard, and the latest *Songbook* translation software."

The SEALs voiced their appreciation of the engineering needed to miniaturize and pressure-proof such complex electronics.

April smiled. "As you all know, dolphins cannot actually speak like humans - they have no vocal cords - but they can certainly communicate volumes of information and ideas. Greg Mason introduced the term *'talking dolphins'* - a metaphor for *Songbook* - a computer-based language translation system he and his team of linguists developed over many years of scientific effort."

"Does the GUI function the same as the older version? I hope the programmers didn't change the icons and move the drop down menus to different locations. It makes the learning curve more like a curse."

"Naturally, there are some additional buttons and menus, but the guys tried to preserve as many legacy features as practical. Remember, none of this would have been possible without the *Songbook* software. You all know the dolphin language lacks syntax and is impossible to translate. Even with the most powerful supercomputers, the language of the dolphin remains an enigma. But after years of research, Greg and his team of linguists discovered the secret to communicating with these magnanimous animals. Rather than attempting to decipher their language - he taught them ours. And now his team has done it again with this new communication tool."

"Is that why you married him?" Wagner joshed.

April giggled and rolled her eyes. "One of many reasons. But let's stay on task. That was three years ago and much has changed - for the better. Today, DARPA is pleased to introduce the DULAN version of the *Songbook* system to the SEAL and EOD community."

"How deep can this thing operate?" asked Chief Pace.

"Fifteen hundred feet."

The SEALs glanced about the room acknowledging the operational potential this new instrument offered.

"Most of you remember from your previous training that there are about twenty thousand words in our active vocabulary. But the actual number of words used in ninety percent of the things we use every day, emails, blogs, conversations, etcetera, is only one thousand. Those words are the most important words in the Dolphinese Dictionary."

"I still have a hard time grasping that," confessed Pace.

"Remember *Green Eggs and Ham* by Doctor Seuss?"

Everyone nodded. They'd heard this story before but it was always a good reminder.

"Well, as I'm sure you've heard before, that story had only fifty different words. And his next book, *The Cat in the Hat,* had only two hundred and twenty-five different words." Chief Pace chuckled.

"Thank you, Doctor Seuss." April looked up at the ceiling as if she was talking to the spirit of Doctor Seuss.

"Will it play animated video graphics?"

"Absolutely. Video, stills, you can even draw a sketch on the screen - all while underwater."

"How many divers and dolphins can be on the network at one time?" asked Chief Wagner.

"The CPU and RAM can support up to six dolphins and six divers - plus topside command and control."

"So the conversation between us, the dolphins, and topside is tracked on the computer screen just like the surface-based *Songbook?*"

"Exactly. Word for word."

"What's the range?"

"Currently about two thousand yards. That's about a mile. We have a more powerful unit in the works. It will be capable of five thousand yards. Naturally, water turbidity and thermals may limit the range depending on whether you're communicating horizontally or vertically through the water column."

"It sounds great. I'm anxious to give it a go."

"Let's take five and meet at the training tank. Uno and Luke are waiting to demonstrate their academic skills. Chiefs Pace and Wagner have volunteered to be the first to try out this new system - but everyone will get to use it today. I'll stay topside and monitor the dialog. .

Larry S. Pace was born in Denver, Colorado, in 1987. He was a gregarious and playful youngster with lots of friends and a gentle disposition. He excelled in athletics, and was voted captain of his high school football team. Every Fourth of July, he could be seen driving around town in his pick-up truck with a couple of his buddies - a large American flag flapping wildly in the breeze. His neighbors will always remember him as the kid who stood up to a couple of hooligans who were teasing a smaller classmate. Without so much as a single punch, he negotiated a truce and made three new friends.

After two years of junior college, he joined the Navy with the goal of becoming a SEAL. Shortly after graduating from boot camp, he was selected to attend BUD/S (Basic Underwater Demolition SEAL) training in Coronado, California, where he graduated with Class 404 in 2008. His courageous performance in Afghanistan, followed by three tours to Libya and Syria, earned him the Navy Cross. Now, after fifteen years in SEAL Team One, he was assigned an Instructor's billet at BUD/S.

Robert O. Wagner was from Minnesota. At six foot four, he excelled in ice hockey and basketball - contact sports demanding courage and endurance. When the war in the Middle East began, he joined the Navy and at the age of twenty-two completed BUD/S in the winter of 2006. Wagner knew the challenges and dangers of being a SEAL - constant training, overseas deployments, never home long enough to fall in love, marry, and settle down. The SEAL way of life is perfect for a globetrotting adrenaline junkie - and in that environment, Wagner thrived.

****

April stood at the edge of the training tank while each SEAL took possession of his composite equipment case containing one of the DULAN systems.

"Okay, men. Watch and follow along with me. Wrap the computer around your wrist, turn on the power and wait for the red light to appear then enter your user name and password. The green light will indicate you're connected to the network. Put on your facemask and adjust the rubber straps to make a tight seal. The transceiver, bone conduction speaker, and microphone are embedded in the rubber. The computer includes a high-speed CPU, sixty-four gigabytes of RAM, a five-inch, high-resolution monitor, and miniature transceiver. The talk-to-text, text-to-talk features use the same icons and control features you learned in basic *Songbook* training."

"Okay, everyone in the water."

With facemasks in place, everyone jumped into the training tank and drifted to the bottom.

April took her place at the *Songbook* control station. "Can everyone hear me?" She asked over the network.

Each SEAL verbally confirmed reception.

"You can enter text on the keypad or speak into the microphone. The computer will translate your input into Dolphinese and transmit the signal to the dolphins via the transceiver. Chief Wagner and Pace, are you ready to communicate with Uno and Luke?"

"Yes, ma'am," Pace and Wagner replied in unison.

"Swim to the center of the tank and ask them the questions we discussed earlier. Everyone else, watch and learn. I'll be video recording this evolution, so smile for the camera and you just might win an Academy Award for the best training film. Uno and Luke are waiting for you. You can communicate with them and me just like you would if you were on deck."

Pace and Wagner swam to the middle of the tank. Luke immediately approached Wagner and rolled onto his side, eager to be scratched on his flanks. Within seconds, Uno nuzzled up to Pace, blew a frothy stream of bubbles and began to communicate.

[UNO] Hello Pace. I see you have a new computer.

[PACE] Hello Uno. Yes. This is a new Songbook system.

[LUKE] Hello April. Did you help design this system?

[APRIL] No. I had little to do with it. Our engineering team created it.

[UNO] Dolphins don't need computers to communicate with other dolphins.

[APRIL] Luke. I want to ask you some questions to test your memory. Chief Pace and Wagner will ask some too.

[LUKE] Please proceed.

[APRIL] How many pounds in a kilogram?

[LUKE] There are two point two pounds per kilogram.

[APRIL] Good. How many inches in a meter?

[LUKE] There are thirty-nine point thirty-seven inches in a meter.

[APRIL] Excellent, Uno. Pace has some questions for you regarding gas physics.

[UNO] I learned all about gas physics several months ago.

[PACE] What is the fundamental principle of Charles's Law?

[UNO] Charles's Law states when the pressure of a gas is held constant, the temperature and volume will be directly related.

[WAGNER] Uno do you have a girlfriend?

[UNO] I have many special female friends. Do you have a female friend?

[WAGNER] I don't have time for female friends. I spend much of my time away from home.

[LUKE] I have a female friend. She will soon have our baby. We are both happy.

[UNO] Dos is my female friend. She has a son named Tres. They live with me in the conservatory. They are smart dolphins.

[WAGNER] Uno. Let's see how well you remember your geometry lessons. What is the equation for computing the volume of a sphere?

[UNO] The volume of a sphere is four thirds times pi times the radius cubed.

[WAGNER] You are correct. I had to look it up before we got in the water.

[UNO] I know.

Startled by Uno's quip, Wagner shrugged his shoulders.

[WAGNER] I don't believe you know the answer to this next question.

[UNO] Try me.

[WAGNER] What is the nominal temperature of our sun?

[UNO] I was born in Denver.

[APRIL] Uno. You are being silly?

[UNO] I was joking with Wagner.

Uno swam a couple of circles while pretending to be thinking. He stopped in front of Wagner for a moment then made another circle.

[APRIL] Come on Uno. I know you have the correct answer.

[UNO] It is very hot. Do you want it in Celsius or Fahrenheit? Never mind. I have the answer in both units. Twenty - seven million degrees Fahrenheit - fifteen million degrees Celsius.

[WAGNER] You are a very smart dolphin. Smile for the camera.

UNO quickly flipped around and began to swim circles around Pace and Wagner while smiling at the camera.

[UNO] Dolphins are always smiling. Do you know why?

[WAGNER] Why?

[UNO] Because we understand your language and you cannot learn ours.

[APRIL] Luke. What time is it?

[LUKE] Time for treats.

[PACE] Uno and Luke. You both did an excellent job.

[UNO] Would you like us to show you more behaviors?

[PACE] That would be a good thing for another day. I will ask April to set that up. I am getting out now. Goodbye Uno. Goodbye Luke.

BERKELEY

Hakeem Rubuka rose from a restless slumber. Memories of the drone attack that killed his father haunted his thoughts.

"Fucking infidels," he muttered. "Allah, please give us the power to rid the world of these non-believers." His heart quickly filled with his daily dose of vengeance.

It was just past seven on a Wednesday morning. Rubbing his eyes, he walked into the small kitchen to prepare his morning meal - black tea, Syrian cheese, olive and tomato halawa paste scooped from his dish with a fresh slice of pita bread.

While waiting for the water to boil, he looked out his second-story kitchen window at the crowded street below. Hundreds of University of California students headed for an early morning class while their minds digested bits and pieces of insignificant tweets, fake news, and minutiae from their smartphones.

Small clusters of foreign students from diverse cultures gathered along Bancroft Way sipping flavored coffee drinks or fruity variations of green tea - tablets and laptops charged and ready for another day of brainwashing in the social egalitarian way of life. Every one of them was a non-believer - an infidel.

Today, however, Hakeem and his brother Ramin had other plans. Hakeem had recently received a BS degree in nuclear physics and was searching for a job. Ramin continued working on his electrical engineering Masters degree.

"Good blessings to you this glorious day, brother," said Hakeem as he walked toward the refrigerator.

"Good morning, Hakeem. What are you up to today - sending out more letters?"

"We've got to meet Abdul at Eastshore Park at ten. He wants to talk to us about a new mission. He insisted you to come with me."

"Abdul. That spoiled brat son of Sheik Mijou al Bagot. That shit bird spends more money a month chasing white pussy than we spend on rent."

"I know he's a bit weird, but his family is wealthy and the Sheik is wise in the ways of jihad. I will never forget what he said many times. 'One day we will run out of oil. That will be the day our world dies.' That's why he wanted us to learn about science and technology - things of the future."

"Yeah, I remember. And that's the reason papa went to work for him - and died for him."

"We'd probably be dead too if it wasn't for Abdul's father. He arranged for our student visas, paid for our education, and gives us money to live in this nice apartment. Everyone in our cell receives a good allowance. Abdul is close to his father - someday he'll inherit his fortune."

"Sure, I'll join you. As much as I dislike that sadistic coke head, he's on our side and we need his father's money to fulfill our destiny."

****

The Rubuka brothers were deeply committed to ISIS jihadist principles, as was their deceased father. They swore an oath to die for the glory of Allah and the caliphate and to do whatever was asked of them to rid the world of non-believers.

Hakeem and Ramin Rubuka were born and raised in Iraq.

Their father, Ismael, was a ranking member of the Ba'athist party and a Deputy Assistant in Saddam Hussein's Revolutionary Council. However, the Americans invaded Baghdad, destroyed their home, and killed their mother and sister, calling their death and destruction "collateral damage."

Ismael and his two sons fled to Saudi Arabia and found refuge within the Sunni Salafi clan of Sheik Mijou al Bagot, a sympathizer to the Ba'ath party and a major financial backer and strategist of ISIS.

ISIS was born out of the U.S. invasion of Iraq in 2003. When America decided to *de-Baathify* the Iraqi civil and military services, hundreds of thousands of Sunnis formerly loyal to Saddam Hussein were left without a job - and they were mad as hell.

Osama bin Laden capitalized on their anger and waged war against America and her allies. His brutal ideology quickly gained traction and migrated to Syria where the leaders changed the name to the Islamic State of Syria - ISIS.

The ISIS ideology was in many ways similar to the Ba'athist. The main supporters of both parties were Sunni Salafi Arabs who preached Islamic jihad. Like Ba'ath, ISIS ideology was strict and uncompromising. Only six days after he was declared president, Ba'athist Saddam Hussein, at a meeting of the Revolutionary Command Council, called out the names of hundreds of men he perceived to be enemies of the state. These men and hundreds more were arrested and summarily executed.

As a disenfranchised Ba'athist, Ismael Rubuka was compelled to work for the Sheik in order to repay him for saving him and his two sons from certain death at the hands of the infidels. To compensate the Sheik for his generosity, the Sheik ordered Ismael to help finance ISIS operations by delivering crude oil into Turkey. It was a dangerous but necessary assignment.

With the help of ISIS leadership, Ismael quickly learned how to travel along the major roadways while talking and bribing his way through shifting security zones. Navigating the fifty-mile route with five thousand gallons of ISIS crude took courage, plenty of cash, and nerves of steel. He would not be alone; a convoy of tanker trucks - often fifty or more - traveled in a long caravan. One or more ISIS pickup trucks carrying half a dozen well-armed ISIS soldiers accompanied the caravan to and from their destination. Nevertheless, there were dangers on the highway and enemy aircraft in the sky.

****

As he continued eating his breakfast, Hakeem recalled the last day he saw his father. It was at the Riyadh airport and Ismael had a one-way ticket to Damascus.

"Come to me, son. Give your papa a big hug. Wish me good fortune. Study hard. Learn your lessons well. Make me proud. Remember to do what is right for Allah and your brother." Ismael gave him a big hug, then turned and walked to the boarding ramp.

Several months later, Hakeem got the shocking news.

As usual, Ismael had driven his Mercedes sedan twenty miles to the Omin pump station. The journey was relatively safe - well guarded by ISIS patrols. Here in Omin, ISIS stored Syrian crude oil until it could be loaded onto private tanker trucks and delivered to international oil traders in Kilis, Turkey.

After hundreds of trips, Ismael knew the drill. Highway D850 led north toward Turkey through checkpoints in and out of Aleppo. Ismael always called ahead to see if there were additional checkpoints in Anadan or Nubl. The last checkpoint was Azaz, four miles south of the Turkish border crossing at Senir Kapisi.

Once he reached the crude storage and pump station, his load of crude would be pumped into ships moored at the Turkish Mediterranean port of Iskenderun. The receiving inspector would weigh his load and give him a receipt. Upon his return to Omin, he would present his receipt to the ISIS cashier and receive his payment, minus fees for the armed guards and pickup truck.

The roadside had been repeatedly bombed by Syrian, Russian, and American jets and drones. Large piles of rubble and blackened bomb pits peppered the landscape. Block after block of homes, apartments, and commercial structures were now heaps of debris and piles of dismembered brick buildings. Burned-out cars, vans, and trucks marked the graves of their drivers and passengers. The stench of smoldering human flesh permeated the air.

Nobody saw it coming. Not the ISIS sentries nor the truckers. The high-altitude Reaper drone was invisible to the naked eye and as stealthy as a cobra. The train of Hellfire missiles seemed to come from outer space.

Ismael's truckload of crude oil exploded high into the northern Syrian sky. Nothing was left but a burning hulk - and the charred remains of the headless driver blown out of the front window.

MEET THE REAPER

"Good evening, Chief. Did you have a nice weekend?"

"Evening, LT. Yeah. I barbequed some baby back ribs for the wife and drank a few beers while we watched the desert sunset. By nine o'clock every star in our galaxy could be seen. It was an awesome sight. How about you?"

"Gail wanted to spend some time in the Bellagio. We had a great buffet and she won a hundred bucks playing Keno. I blew fifty at blackjack, but we enjoyed watching the crowd. I can't believe how much money the Asians spend at the slots and tables. They must all be millionaires. Are we all set to rock and roll?" asked Lieutenant Simon.

"Yes, sir. You've been assigned Reaper twenty-two. All systems check out. She's fueled, armed, and ready for take-off." It was eight p.m. in Nevada - six in the morning at the Incirlik Air Base in eastern Turkey.

From Las Vegas, the top secret Reaper Mission Control building was a one-hour drive down a dirt road in a four-wheel drive desert vehicle. The portable control room consisted of a forty-foot-long, air-conditioned metal container with sufficient space for four two-man teams. Each of the four pilots paired with a senior enlisted weapons systems specialist.

The pilot controlled the Reaper via a joystick equipped with numerous buttons: one for communications with the ground crew at Incirlik, another to speak with a forward observer, a third for firing a Hellfire air to ground missile, a GBU-12 or GBU-38 JDAM smart bomb. Sitting next to the pilot, the weapons specialist controlled the laser target designator and selected the appropriate weapon for the mission.

Lieutenant Simon was one of two dozen Air Force drone pilots assigned to the facility. He and his partner, Chief Salazar, sat in air-conditioned comfort, staring at rows of brightly lit lights, data screens and several high-resolution video feeds - one for aerial navigation, another looking down and zoomed onto the target, a third showing the Reaper drone on the runway - 7,200 miles away.

Even at the maximum cruise altitude of 40,000 feet, the laser-guided ordnance could hit a five-meter-wide target ninety percent of the time. Capable of staying aloft for up to thirty hours, the Reaper quickly earned a reputation for destroying enemy tanks, buildings, and armored vehicles. It was especially revered for its ability to destroy ISIS crude oil tanker trucks. It was the perfect hunting and killing machine - powerful, stealthy, deadly even on fleeing or time-sensitive targets.

"Incirlik, this is Reaper twenty-two. I have visual control. Request permission to depart."

"Reaper twenty-two, you are cleared for takeoff. Air temperature is twenty degrees Celsius. Wind five to ten knots out of the south. Good luck."

"Roger."

Lieutenant Simon pushed the throttle forward and released the brakes. His instruments flickered as the engine gained power, then, within a few seconds, the Reaper accelerated down the runway.

"Thirty knots... forty... fifty..." Chief Salazar called out the ground speed. When the ground speed reached sixty knots, Lieutenant Simon pulled back the joystick and watched the instrument panel to confirm it was climbing skyward at a steep, forty-five- degree angle.

"Where we headed today, LT?" asked Salazar.

"Where do you think, Chief?"

"Aleppo to Kilis. That's the most likely route for ISIS tankers."

"Roger that. You can unlock the Hellfire missiles. We'll be over the kill zone in twenty minutes."

Sitting in front of a couple of flat screen video monitors, remotely maneuvering a drone traveling three hundred miles an hour seven thousand miles away is not like any other type of flying - especially if you were trained to fly in the cockpit of F-15s and F-22 Raptors. Now that was flying. Controlling an unmanned drone over enemy territory - well, that was more like gaming.

"LT, check this out!" said Chief Salazar pointing to one of the monitors. "We've got ourselves a turkey shoot. There must be thirty tanker trucks in that convoy." Droplets of perspiration burst from Salazar's forehead.

"Holy shit! I better call for back-up. We're gonna need help. I'm calling the Colonel."

Lieutenant Simon selected the secure com line and called his commanding officer.

The Colonel answered on the second ring tone.

"Sorry to disturb you, sir, but we've got a tanker convoy in our sights - maybe thirty targets. We've got four Hellfire missiles and with any luck can kill a half dozen. We could sure use another bird or two - do some real damage to these ISIS pricks."

"I'll do what I can. Go ahead and engage the lead targets. That should slow down the convoy and give us a chance to bring in more firepower."

"Yes, sir."

Turning to Chief Salazar, Simon said, "We might get some help. I'm engaging the lead truck now. Paint the lead truck and record the action."

"Roger. Video recorder on. Laser painting the lead truck."

"Fire number one."

Chief Salazar pushed the ignition button for Hellfire number one. The Reaper bounced upward a few inches as the missile erupted from under the port wing.

"Missile away. Twelve seconds to impact."

The men watched the video from the nose camera of the Hellfire as it raced toward the lead truck at fifteen hundred feet per second.

The shockwave from the explosion temporarily saturated the camera and distorted the screen image.

"Bingo! We got the lead truck. She exploded and knocked out the second truck. Okay, let's paint the third truck."

"Painting truck number three."

"Fire missile number two."

"Missile away. Twelve seconds to impact."

"Bingo! Bango! Bongo! Another one bites the dust." Simon swayed his upper torso and waved his arms in the air.

"Paint number five and fire when ready." Both men felt the rush of adrenaline as it poured into their brains.

"Goddamn, this is fun. Better than the Wheel of Fortune at Caesar's Palace."

"Holy shit! Did you see that? Damn truck blew twenty feet into the air. Fucking headless driver flew clean through the front window - one giant flaming asshole."

"Paint the next truck and fire when ready."

"Missile away."

"Reaper twenty-two, this is Reaper forty-one. We're coming in for some fun. Hope you left a few targets for us. Nice shooting."

"Reaper forty-one, this is twenty-two. Welcome to the party. Where are you located?"

"Wichita, Kansas."

"Good luck, forty-one. We're outta here."

DJINNI

"Come on, Ramin. Hurry. We're late."

"Sorry, I just had to have a double espresso - kick-start the brain."

"Eight dollars for a double. Those baristas must earn a small fortune."

"I'd like to screw the blonde," muttered Ramin.

"You just might get to do that if you die a martyr. Allah promised us a sensual paradise - seventy-two horny virgins and a perpetual hard-on. And, you'll live forever with an insatiable appetite for virgins with large, pear-shaped breasts."

"Allahu Akbar."

"Hurry. Abdul said he'd meet us at the concrete bench overlooking the lake. We've got a three-mile walk."

The Rubuka brothers hustled down University Avenue, took the pedestrian tunnel under Interstate 580 and followed the footpath to the shoreline of the Eastshore Park Lake. They found the concrete bench and took a seat.

"I wonder what Abdul wants to talk about. It must be something important. He said it came from the top. I assume he means the Sheik," said Hakeem.

"He certainly knows how to leverage his pedigree. Fucking playboy."

Hakeem sensed the hostility in his brother's voice. Maybe it was jealousy.

"Be polite. He's an important asset. We need him as much as he needs us."

"I know. But it makes me angry - all his fancy cars and women fawning over him." Ramin scanned the lake, observing a couple of radio-controlled sailboats on a southerly tack, their young skippers running up and down the concrete perimeter.

"See that man. He's heading this way. The tall guy, dressed in a dark suit."

"Yeah, I see him. He's got a black patch over his left eye. Looks like a hit man to me," said Ramin jokingly.

"He's looking right at us. Now he's looking around for other people. I wonder what he's up to."

"Just be cool."

The man stopped in front of Hakeem and his brother. Holding his head high, he slowly turned a full circle while scanning the surrounding grounds and shoreline. Upon completing a full turn, he stopped and looked down at Hakeem.

"I assume you are Hakeem Rubuka," he said, while his right eye scanned the faces of the Rubuka brothers.

"Yes, and this is my brother, Ramin. What do you want?"

"I'm here on behalf of the Sheik and his son Abdul. I am his emissary. Stand and let me pat you down for weapons and wires."

The brothers looked at each other and shrugged. "Sure, why not?"

After he completed his search, he ordered them to sit.

"Make a space. I'll sit in the middle." The brothers parted to make room for the mystery man.

"What's your name?" asked Ramin.

"Djinni," he replied, without looking at Ramin.

"Djinni. Isn't that the name of a magical spirit with supernatural power?" asked Hakeem.

"I live in Dubai. While I work alone, I am not alone. There

are many others like me around the world." Djinni drilled his lone gray eye into the eyes of Hakeem, then flashed a steely glance toward Ramin.

Hakeem blinked twice and squinted. "What brings you to Berkeley?"

"The Sheik has a special mission for you. Have you been trained in scuba diving?"

"No, we've been busy attending university. Why do you ask?"

"You are both registered to take a scuba diving course in San Diego. You'll be there for about four weeks. All your equipment and course materials are pre-paid. You'll be staying at the Mission Bay Apartments on Midway Avenue. There is a rental car waiting when you arrive. Here are your tickets and some cash."

"Scuba diving? I'm not a very good swimmer," Ramin said with trepidation. "In fact, I hate cold water."

"Get over it. This is essential to your mission for ISIS, the caliphate - for Allah."

"Allahu Akbar," said Hakeem.

"Oh, and one more thing. You need to shave your face. We don't want to raise any suspicion and it will be easier to seal your facemask against smooth skin."

****

"What are we doing with all this dive gear? This shit must weigh fifty kilos." Ramin continued his grumblings, searching for a way out of the scuba dive training program. "The fucking water is freezing cold too."

"That's what the wetsuit is for, to keep you warm. Come on, Ramin. Don't be a crybaby. Focus on the objective. We've been called by Allah for a special mission and I'm not going to fail. Now get your ass in that rubber suit and follow the instructor into the water."

****

"We've completed the basic open water phase, diver diseases, and rescue diver phases. We've got one more class - wreck diving - and we'll be certified," said Hakeem.

"Brrr. How deep is the wreck?" asked Ramin. "I'm not feeling well. My head hurts."

"Come on, Ramin. It's the last dive. It's an old sunken destroyer. There will be lots of fish, and maybe a harbor seal or two. Come on, man. You're going to get through it just fine. Follow me. I'll show you the way."

Even though he was the younger brother, Hakeem felt obliged to help Ramin work his way through the anger and anguish of a jihadist's life.

"What'll we do after we get certified?"

"We're going to take a course in underwater propulsion systems - dive scooters. They pull you through the water so you don't have to use your fins. It sounds like fun. We can cruise through the kelp beds and chase some leopard sharks."

"Okay, I'll do it for you, but I won't like it."

****

"Hakeem, wake up. There's someone knocking on our door. Wake up. Who could be calling on us at this time of day?"

"What time is it? It's still dark outside." The men heard more knocks.

"Ramin, go see who it is."

Ramin nervously walked to the door of their apartment and called out, "Who's there? What do you want?"

"It's Djinni. Open the door!"

"Sorry, I didn't know. Give me a second to unlock it. Come on in." Djinni didn't look at Ramin as he rushed into the bedroom.

"Get up and get dressed. There are some people you need to meet."

"Where are we going? What's happening?"

"You'll see. Get dressed. We're driving to a coffee house in

National City. Meet me curbside. You have fifteen minutes."

****

Djinni was standing at the driver side door of his extended cab truck when the Rubuka brothers arrived.

"Sit in the back, both of you," he ordered.

"Where are we going?" asked Hakeem.

"To a coffee house - and I don't like repeating myself."

They drove in silence to a small coffee house on National City Boulevard, just opposite the US Naval Shipyard. The sign said it was closed but Djinni unlocked the door and waved for the brothers to join him in the dimly lit shop. Djinni closed and locked the door.

"Sit here. I'll be right back."

Moments later, Djinni appeared, followed by three scruffy men. He pushed another table close to the brothers, motioning for everyone to be seated.

"These are your Chechen Muslim brothers - new members of your cell." The Chechen men remained stoic and did not offer a hand to shake.

"Left to right, this is Ziad, Khalid, and Osaman. They are all veterans of the war on the infidels and skilled divers - demolition saboteurs and underwater jihadists. Let's get some coffee and talk. We have much to consider."

****

Ninety-five percent of the citizens of the Chechen Republic were Sunni Muslims. Shortly after the collapse of the Soviet Union, the country declared independence.

Determined to keep the Chechens under communist political influence, the Russians invaded - killing over 200,000 Muslim citizens - leaving a legacy of ashes and thousands of orphaned children including Ziad, Khalid and Osaman.

Ziaid was a hot tempered youngster, often getting into fist

fights with older orphans and known to be a petty thief by local merchants. His father was arrested and murdered by the KGB at the start of the Grozny invasion. After graduating from secondary school, Ziad joined the fight for global Muslim dominance and quickly earned a reputation for egregious jihad. He specialized in IED and booby traps.

Khalid came from an upper middle-class family and had dreamt of becoming a doctor. His father was an engineer in the Grozny public works department. Both parents were killed in a bombing raid during the second Russian invasion. He was adopted by an uncle and indoctrinated in the ways of jihad by a local Sunni imam. He later joined an ISIS cell specializing in underwater demolition and volunteered to come to America to destroy the non-believers.

Osaman was the only surviving member of his family. Russian artillery killed his mother and two sisters while they shopped in the marketplace. Russian tanks destroyed his home and killed his father and two younger brothers while he was at school. When he turned sixteen, he was recruited and radicalized by ISIS and volunteered to bring jihad to America.

****

Everyone took a sip or two of their coffee before Djinni continued.

"I'm sure everyone here has heard about the Fukushima nuclear power plant meltdown back in 2011. A fifty-foot tsunami killed the electrical power to the cooling pumps, causing the reactors to melt down. Thousands of people died as a direct result of the explosions and radiation exposure. Five hundred thousand have succumbed to radiation-induced cancer since the incident. The city of Tokyo will begin evacuations within the next five years. It can't be stopped."

"Allahu Akbar," said Ziad.

Djinni continued, slowly enunciating his strategic message.

"The meltdown created a no life zone over a fifty-mile radius. That's about four thousand square miles around the plant."

Djinni waited for the Chechens to react. Ziad gazed at Khalid and shrugged his shoulders. Gritting their teeth, the Rubuka brothers acknowledged the massive power and destructive force of a nuclear reactor meltdown.

"Since then, the no life zone has expanded to a hundred miles from ground zero - fifteen thousand square miles."

Khalid, raised his eyes while computing the math. "Eight hundred times the size of Grozny, our capital city."

Everyone leaned closer, beginning to realize where Djinni was headed with his briefing. Djinni broke out a map, placed it on the table and scanned the faces of his warriors.

"Look at this map. It's the Ortega nuclear power plant, sixty miles north of downtown San Diego. Your primary mission is to destroy the cooling water pumps - the same kind of cooling pumps that were disabled by the tsunami at Fukushima."

Ramin looked at his brother and snickered. "What a great way to fuck over the infidels."

"This will cause a massive meltdown. Tens of thousands of non-believers will die."

"Allahu Akbar."

"But that's not all. Over the next ten years, the radiation will doom the population centers of southern California. From San Diego to Ventura - every town, village, and community will slowly turn into a no life zone. Thirty million infidels live within this area." Djinni paused to reflect on the enormity of their heinous mission.

"Hakeem, as a nuclear physicist you know the killing power of nuclear radiation. Please tell us what the infidels of southern California can expect."

"Gamma radiation is the most deadly. It causes mutations in DNA and damages cellular mechanisms. In large doses, it kills all living cells and causes radiation poisoning. Much of the destruction will depend on the prevailing winds. Each isotope has different properties. Iodine-131 exposure causes thyroid cancer but it has a short half-life - only eight days. Caesium-137 is a major threat because it is absorbed throughout the body and has a half-life of thirty years. Exposure to gamma radiation occurs through ingestion or inhalation and causes cancer to invade muscles."

"How much gamma radiation is needed to kill an infidel?" asked Ramin.

"Not much, but it depends on several factors such as the dosage, clothing, immune system, age, and duration of exposure. The real monsters hang around for a long time. For the infidels, it's the gift that keeps on giving."

The Chechens emitted a malevolent chuckle.

"And what are these monsters?" asked Djinni with a satanic grin.

"Strontium-90 and Plutonium-239. Strontium-90 attacks the bones and blood-forming tissues and has a half-life of thirty years. Plutonium-239 has a half-life of 24,000 years. These killers are eternal," said Hakeem.

Everyone looked around the table, grateful to Allah for choosing them for this mission.

"Let's take a short break, hit the latrine, and grab another cup of coffee. This next session will get to the tactical details."

CHECKMATE

"What time is it?" April yawed and stretched out her arms like a soaring eagle.

"Almost eight o'clock. It's Saturday, and we slept in. I have a surprise for us," Greg snuggled and whispered in April's ear.

"Darling, I love your surprises."

"You know it's our third anniversary next month. So I thought about making reservations at the new Royal Chateau in Grand Bahama. We've never been there before. I hear they have the most magnificent ocean view suites in the world and thick, down-filled comforters - the squishy kind you can sink into up to your ears."

"Nothing is more enticing than being in bed with my man." April wiggled her fanny into Greg's abdomen while he tenderly held her close.

"We can spend a week relaxing by the pool or scuba diving or whatever. They've got seven swimming pools and a wonderful snorkeling reef. We can rent a boat if you want to do some exploring - maybe find a secluded beach - someplace where we can be alone and celebrate three wonderful years together."

"That would be fabulous. We need some private time - no midnight phone calls. When do we leave?"

"I'll call the travel agent."

"Shucks, honey, that gives us plenty of time to practice. Come to me, lover boy." April rolled over to face Greg and began her ritual massage. "Wanna fiddle around before breakfast?"

"Fiddle, faddle, jump in the saddle," Greg chuckled.

"Silly poet. We have so much fun in bed. It's the happiest place in my world. Do you like that?" Their passion deepened.

"Oh, yeah. Can't you see you're driving me crazy." Greg moved closer and they exchanged a long, luscious kiss.

April pulled off the covers and rested her head on Greg's chest.

"I could stay here forever. I'm so happy. You make my life so complete. I love you so much." Slowly, she sat upright and gave Greg a sultry pose. "This is such a beautiful place to love the man of my dreams. Do you think we can stay forever?"

"Forever is a long time. Who knows what's ahead. Let's enjoy what we have - live in the moment. It's ours now - let's not worry about the future. Besides, neither of us has a crystal ball. We can chart a course but the winds and tides may not take us there."

"I know. You're a realist. But I can dream and you can too. So give me a kiss and I'll make you happy."

"Sweetie pie, you always make me happy." She squeezed him seductively. "How about a little revelry before breakfast?"

Greg was spellbound by her charms.

"Just lie back and enjoy." She swirled the tip of her tongue across her lips until they shone in the morning sunlight, then with a yearning smile gazed down and purred, "Pour moi?" She coyly raised her eyebrows and puckered her wet lips.

"Oui, pour mon amour."

"Hmm. Yummy! I'm going to take you to a magical place," she cooed.

"What about you?"

"I'm just going to warm you up. You know I love you best when your heart beats deep inside me."

****

Greg had just finished showering when his cell phone rang.

"Good morning, Ricky. What's up at the conservatory?"

"Sorry to disturb you and April but I thought you should know about our recent developments with Uno." Ricky's voice held the promise of something special.

"Go on. What's the news?"

"Well, you are aware of our phase two cognitive skills assessment exercises for our adult dolphins. We've been working with Uno testing his problem solving and decision-making skills."

"I sure am. Come on, Ricky. Speak up, man."

"You may want to sit down."

"Damn, Ricky. Talk to me."

"Uno beat me at a game of chess - not once - but three straight games!"

****

David Stratton, Executive Director of DARPA, answered his phone on the first ring tone.

"Hello, Greg. Good to hear from you."

"David, we've made a significant breakthrough in our dolphin cognitive assessment research. It's mind-blowing stuff. I think you should come down to witness this landmark discovery. We've got it on video and classified it top secret. It would be good if Admiral Dobbins and General Goodson from the Pentagon could join you, as well as the appropriate heads of DHS, FBI, CIA, and NSA."

"What about Allan Rusk, our West Coast conservatory director? He should be there too."

"Absolutely. We'll need his expertise in developing applications. I'll invite him personally. We're good friends - go back a long way. He'll appreciate knowing he got the news first-hand."

"When and where do you want to meet?"

"DARPA, Cape Canaveral - we'll gather in the conservatory seaquarium. What's your schedule for the next few weeks?"

"I'm usually free, but let me check in with the others and call you back."

"Great, April and I look forward to seeing you."

****

The conservatory seaquarium consisted of a two-million-gallon indoor tank with a bulletproof, sixteen-foot-high glass enclosure. Rows of variable-intensity white and blue lights lined the perimeter. Several LCD video monitors faced the inside of the tank viewable by the dolphins and divers.

At the far end of the aquarium, a walkway led to a swim-up platform. Here, the trainers handed out rewards and tended to the dolphins up close and personal.

Rows of comfortable chairs surrounded the tank providing ample seating and a bird's eye view of the action for dignitaries and special visitors.

Directly above the guest seating, an eighty-four-inch, super-high-resolution LCD flat panel display hung from the ceiling, allowing the *Songbook* operator and visitors to see the text exchange between the dolphins and operator. Numerous video cameras were conveniently positioned both above and below the water. Everything was recorded and classified.

Most impressive was the surround-sound speaker system. During a conversation between a human and a dolphin, the *Songbook* software converted the English and Dolphinese conversation into text and displayed it on the monitor. At the same time, the computer converted the text into synthetic voices matching the gender and personality characteristics of each party to the conversation. To the audience, it was like watching and hearing an English-speaking movie *with English subtitles*.

****

Greg welcomed his guests. "Good morning, gentlemen, and welcome to DARPA. I'd like to introduce you to Barry Kasorovski, the gentleman sitting next to me."

Barry stood and waved his hand at the dignified guests.

"He's offered to help us with this demonstration. Two months ago, in London, he beat the pants off dozens of world class chess players to win the International Chess Championship. Please give him a warm welcome."

The guests applauded appropriately, wondering what the heck was about to transpire. Admiral Dobbins leaned close to David. "Any idea what the hell is going on?"

"Greg said it was a breakthrough in dolphin cognitive research. That's all I know, but he's never disappointed us so I suggest we sit back and enjoy the show."

Greg continued. "We appreciate your visit and hope to show you an amazing performance by one of our most intelligent dolphins. His name is Uno. Uno is a ten-year-old male Atlantic bottlenose dolphin. I believe he will both amaze and mystify your senses. April Tanner, our Director of Training, will operate the *Songbook* communication system. So, sit back, get comfortable and follow the action on the overhead monitor."

Greg took a seat next to April and gave her a big smile, then leaned into her ear and whispered. "Wanna bet who wins?"

"Ten bucks says Uno wins."

"You're on. But let's make it interesting - twenty and a midnight swim."

"You know that's an offer I can't refuse." April giggled and turned to her control console.

The white lights dimmed to complete darkness while the arena filled with Beethoven's Fifth Symphony. Seconds later, a ring of powerful underwater spotlights illuminated Uno as he entered the main tank. He completed two full runs around the perimeter, his massive tail flukes pulsing up and down to the beat of the music. He then approached the viewing audience, leaped high into the air, and blew out a stream of bubbles. The guests welcomed him with loud applause while reading the voice to text conversation on the monitor.

[APRIL] Hello Uno. How are you?

[UNO] Very well thank you. And how are you today April?

[APRIL] Excellent. Are you ready to play a game of chess?

[UNO I love to play chess. Who is my opponent?

[APRIL] Barry Kasorovski, the gentleman sitting at the chess table. He has just returned from London where he won the International Chess Championship.

[UNO] Barry. Nice to meet you. May I call you by your first name?

Barry nodded his approval.

April had briefed Barry on the nature of this demonstration but he had no idea it would be so surreptitious. He was required to submit a full dossier on his background, where and when he was born, what passports he held, where he had lived for the past twenty-five years, and four additional pages of questions, all needed to gain approval to play a game of chess *with a dolphin*.

He recalled April's offer. "If you win the match, we'll give you a cashier's check for twenty-five thousand dollars. If you lose, we'll pick up your expenses and give you five thousand dollars for your time."

Naturally, he had accepted the deal.

April addressed the dignified guests. "Gentlemen, please direct your attention to the monitor. Here you'll see a digital chess board with white and black pieces properly arranged. You can follow the game move by move. For those of you who know the game, you can follow each move in algebraic notation. Each player will call out his move. Uno will go first."

Contemplating his game plan, Barry moved closer to the electronic chess board.

[UNO] Pawn to e4

[BARRY] Pawn to c5

[UNO] Knight to f3

[BARRY] Knight to f6

"Looks like Uno is setting up a Sicilian attack." Greg knew he was going to lose his bet. But a midnight dip with his lovely wife April was a welcome booby prize.

[UNO] Pawn to c3

[BARRY] Pawn to e6

[UNO] Pawn to d4

[BARRY] Pawn captures Pawn at d4

Even after capturing one of Uno's pawns, Barry sensed he was in trouble.

Admiral Dobbins recognized the Sicilian strategy. He leaned closer to General Goodson and whispered. "Can you believe this?"

"Whew! Never in a million years." General Goodson shook his head in disbelief.

"Barry better watch out. Uno knows his game. He's being very aggressive." Admiral Dobbins was mystified by the magic and began to contemplate incredible possibilities.

[UNO] Pawn captures Knight at c3

"Shit." The audience heard Barry cuss.

[BARRY] Bishop to f8

Barry began to shake. Bubbles of perspiration broke through his forehead. His temples began to pound at the prospect of losing to a dolphin. How could this be happening to me? The tension in the room thickened.

[UNO] Knight captures Pawn at e6

Barry shook his head.

[BARRY] Queen to b6

Admiral Dobbins sighed. "It's over." A couple of other guests agreed.

"Yeah, I think he's had it," mumbled Allan.

[UNO] Knight to c7 Checkmate.

Admiral Dobbins gasped, not quite believing his own eyes.

General Goodson shook his head in disbelief.

Allan Rusk took it in stride. He'd seen these kinds of advancements in human-dolphin interaction before. It was always an exciting moment to bring our two species closer together.

"Congratulations Uno!" Barry bowed his head in defeat. "I'd have never - never in a million years thought this was possible." Looking at April he pleaded, "You're not going to issue a press release, are you? I'd be the laughingstock of the chess world."

"There won't be any press release. This is a classified test. We both signed a non-disclosure agreement. Here is your check. We certainly appreciate your cooperation."

"How about a rematch?"

"We'll call you, Mr. Kasorovski. Let me escort you to the exit," said April.

The Pentagon guests were spellbound, trying to fathom what they had just witnessed. The room soon filled with rambling thoughts of how this breakthrough could be used in real world applications.

SAND

"Okay, I understand we need to shut down the cooling pumps, but how do we make a tsunami?" asked Ziad.

"We don't need a tsunami, and believe it or not, we need electrical power to keep the pumps running - at least for a short time."

"I don't understand." Ziad shook his bewildered head.

"Take a good look at this drawing." Djinni unrolled the drawing while the men held the corners in place. "It's a detailed engineering schematic of the cooling system."

"Where in the hell did you find this?" asked Hakeem.

"The Internet. The infidels put everything on the Internet. All you gotta do is ask Mr. Googlebutt."

"These fuckheads are dumber than cockroaches." Khalid shook his head.

"Let's start with the cooling water induction pipe. This is your point of entry. It's big enough to drive a truck through - eighteen feet in diameter. The entrance is located in thirty-five feet of water. It brings in cold seawater from the ocean. The opening extends thirty-two hundred feet to the pump room." Djinni pointed to the pumps.

"It looks like there are two pumps. What's this thing here?" Hakeem pointed to the drawing. "It says it's a rotating biological intervention screen. How do we get past this contraption?"

"You don't."

"How are we supposed to destroy the pumps?"

"Sand."

"Sand? Just ordinary sand? I'm confused." Hakeem struggled to imagine how this plan could work.

"Sand?" Osaman chuckled, thinking Djinni must be joking.

"Yes, it's as simple as sand. You see, as the induction pipe approaches the power plant it is buried under several feet of sand." Djinni traced his finger from the surf zone to the pump chamber. "You don't need to get into the pump chamber - just blow a hole in the top of the pipe in the surf zone. The sand and ocean waves will do the rest."

"How much sand?" asked Khalid.

"More than you can imagine," replied Djinni.

"How big a hole in the pipe?" asked Ramin.

"Three feet square."

Ramin turned on his mental calculator to get a rough estimate of the volume of sand that would gush into the pipe.

Djinni continued with the scenario. "The sand will immediately flood the induction pipe and be sucked into the cooling pumps. Within a couple of minutes, the impellers and bearings will freeze up and trigger a circuit breaker. The pumps will no longer run with sand in them." Djinni exuded arrogant confidence. "Imagine dumping a sack of sand into your garbage disposal." Djinni explored the faces of his jihadists.

"It would destroy the impeller and bearings and burn up the motor," replied Ramin.

"Have you ever seen what sand does to a high-speed vertical pump?" Djinni grimaced and gritted his teeth. "Sand and pumps don't mix."

"What if they have spare parts?" Osaman remained dubious.

"Not a chance. Impeller and bearing replacement takes days and can only be accomplished one pump at a time while the other pump remains operating at full capacity to keep both reactors cool. They've never planned on both pumps going down at once."

Ramin began to verbalize his calculations. "Volume equals pi times the radius squared times the depth divided by three."

"Are you really calculating the sand volume?"

"Give me a second." Unable to finish the calculations in his head, Ramin wrinkled his brow as he completed the solution on his tablet. "I assume the natural flow of saturated sand will yield an obtuse angle of about one hundred and twenty degrees. This will…" Ramin kept punching numbers into his tablet. "Radius twenty feet squared… ten feet below the surface…"

"Come on, man. What's the answer?" Ziad was agitated.

"Two thousand cubic feet a minute - even more with each wave. I'd guess about fifteen thousand cubic feet within the first hour. That's thirty thousand bags of sand."

The men paused and cringed, mouths wide open, astonished at the staggering amount of sand that would flood into the pipe and cooling water pumps.

With the arrogance of a victorious Genghis Khan, Djinni scanned the faces of his operatives, looking for any incertitude.

Djinni declared the obvious. "Nothing will stop the reactors from a complete meltdown!"

Everyone looked at each other, overjoyed to the point of being giddy.

"Death and destruction to the infidels."

"I had no idea it would be so simple," said Ziad, nodding his appreciation of the concept.

"This will be the biggest jihad in the history of ISIS. We'll all be heroes. Papa would be proud," proclaimed Hakeem.

Djinni continued his briefing.

"Linear shape charges will be used to blast a three-foot-square hole in the concrete wall of the pipeline. Using your propulsion units, you'll carry the explosives and tools down the pipe until you are directly under the surf zone."

"What's a linear shape charge?" Hakeem asked.

"Same as a round one - the infidels call them IEDs, improvised explosive devices. Instead of being round and packed into the nose of a 105 Howitzer shell, or an armor piercing RPG, the explosive material runs the length of a rectangular tube. There is a watertight triangular-shaped space in front of the charge. The kinetic energy of a two-inch-wide linear shape charge will cut through ten inches of concrete and two inches of steel." Djinni scowled. "You should read up on this stuff."

The Chechens chuckled at Djinni's brusque reply, then gave Hakeem an insolent frown.

"What is the mission timeline?" inquired Osaman.

Djinni smiled. He had done his homework. "There is a one-knot incoming current. Your propulsion unit can travel at three knots. Do the math. Add the current to the propulsion speed and what do you get?"

"Four knots!" Ziad exclaimed proudly.

"Where'd you learn to count so high?" Osaman smacked Ziad on the top of his head.

"Okay, Osaman. At four knots, how long will it take you to travel twenty-eight hundred feet - rounded up to the nearest minute?"

"Fuck if I know. I need a calculator and the equation for converting knots to feet per second."

"One knot equals one point seven feet per second." Djinni glared at Osaman. "Can you do simple arithmetic?"

Osaman fumbled with the numbers but was unable to calculate the time.

"Eight minutes. That's how long it should take from the time you enter the pipe."

Puzzled, Ziad lowered his head and continued to play with the numbers.

"Okay, Hakeem. Now, how long will it take to return?"

"About fourteen minutes."

"Thank you, Hakeem. Let's figure ten minutes from the time you enter the pipe until you reach the demolition site. Another twenty minutes to secure the linear shape charge and twenty minutes to return against the incoming current. You'll be in and out in less than an hour."

"How will we know we're under the surf zone? GPS won't work underwater," asked Ramin.

"A spool of nylon string with a piece of black cloth tied off twenty-eight hundred feet from the entrance. When you see the black flag, you're directly under the surf zone." Frustrated at the seemingly stupid questions, Djinni gave Ramin a hard stare.

"The shaped charge consists of four sections. Two curved sections conform to the curvature of the pipe; the other two sections are straight. When the four pieces are connected end to end at right angles, they form a three-foot square. This is what you'll attach to the ceiling of the pipe."

"How do we attach this shaped charge to the inside of a pipeline made of steel?" queried Osaman.

"Magnets!" Djinni was quick to reply. "Not just any old refrigerator magnet. I'm talking about neodymium magnets - rare earth magnets. They're the strongest magnets on earth. Ziad, you, Osaman, and Khalid will assemble the linear shape charge while Hakeem and Ramin secure each corner with a magnet. They'll make a metal on metal sound the instant they clamp down to the steel pipe, but not enough to draw the attention of the infidels."

Hakeem was puzzled. "Wait a second. We also have to remain in position while rigging the explosives. There's a one-knot current - maybe more. That's almost two feet per second?"

"Don't worry. Each of you will have a personal magnet and a short piece of rope with a carabiner at each end. One end of the rope will be attached to your harness, the other to the magnet. As soon as you arrive at the demo site, you'll attach your magnet to the inside wall of the steel pipe. It will hold you in position while you attach the shaped charge. When you're ready to exit, disconnect the rope and swim back to the entrance. I'll be waiting to pick you up. No one will ever know you were there."

"How big is this thing?" asked Ramin.

Djinni reached into his backpack and retrieved one of the magnets. Handing it to Ramin he continued. "You can see it's about the size of a hockey puck." Ramin rubbed his fingers over the polished surface and passed it around for the others to inspect. "Be careful. It can crush your fingers if you get too close to a steel object."

"This sucker is heavy for its size," said Hakeem.

"That one-pound magnet has a clamping force of two hundred pounds. Once it's attached, it cannot be removed without a special pry bar."

Ramin nervously raised his hand to ask another question.

"What don't you understand?" Djinni barked.

"I don't think we'll have enough air to complete the task. We'll need to bring extra tanks."

"You're not going to use open circuit scuba - too many bubbles and very noisy. Tomorrow you'll learn how to dive with an oxygen re-breather closed circuit rig - no bubbles, no noise and four hours of dive time on one small tank of oxygen. Meet me at the Mission Bay docks at eight tomorrow morning."

****

The Rubuka brothers arrived on time. The Chechens were twenty minutes late. Djinni was pissed.

"Hey, shitheads. I said eight o'clock. You're twenty minutes late. The next time you pull that shit I'll send you back to Grozny and let your cell boss know you're not worthy of our cause. Now put on your wetsuits and check out your propulsion units."

"Ramin, cast off my bow line. Hakeem, you get the stern. We're headed out to the kelp beds."

Djinni maneuvered the Grady-White cabin cruiser away from the Mission Bay docks and pointed her nose west, down the ship channel toward the open sea. The twin two-fifties would not roar to full power until they cleared the "no wake zone."

"Hang on! We've got some big incoming swells." *Lionfish* rose up the slope of the next big swell, paused for a second, then crashed hard against the lee side of the wave sending an avalanche of seawater over the bow.

"Fuck this shit, man. The water is cold."

"Stop complaining. You're starting to get on my nerves."

Djinni headed away from the channel and turned toward Point Loma. Southeasterly swells were running four to six feet - standing upright became a challenging act of balance.

As they approached the kelp beds, Djinni cut back the power and let *Lionfish* settle to dead slow while he searched for a convenient opening in the kelp.

"You've got to be careful diving in this kelp," he said. "The strands are anchored to the bottom. Many divers have died here."

"Why couldn't they escape? It's just a bunch of weeds."

"They panicked and made it worse, got tangled up in the leafy strands and ran out of air while struggling to free themselves. Didn't they teach you that in your dive class?"

"I guess so. I don't remember it being like this," said Ramin, gesturing at the maze of undulating brown kelp.

"Okay, this is a good spot." Djinni killed the engines and dropped the anchor in a small opening in the middle of a huge patch of kelp. "Your oxygen re-breathers are lined up along the gunnels. Everyone pay close attention. Your life will depend on what I am about to tell you." The mood suddenly thickened.

"We all breathe air. Air is twenty percent oxygen - this is what fuels our bodies. The balance is nitrogen. Nitrogen is inert - colorless, odorless, tasteless. It can also be narcotic if you dive deeper than a hundred feet."

"We know all about gas physics and nitrogen narcosis. It's called rapture of the deep," barked Ziad.

Djinni pointed his solitary eye at Ziad and gritted his teeth with a grinding noise.

"Shut up and listen. Not everyone here is as smart as you think you are."

"Sorry." Ziad looked at his compatriots and shrugged.

Djinni looked at the Rubuka brothers. "You need to pay close attention. Don't let this asshole Ziad get in your head. Diving with pure oxygen is perfectly safe - as long as you do not dive deeper than ten meters. Below ten meters, thirty-three feet is the kill zone - oxygen becomes deadly. It will oxidize your brain and you'll be dead in a matter of seconds!"

"Fuck!" exclaimed Ramin.

"You don't want to die like that," replied Djinni. "You need to know one other thing about this re-breather. There is a valve on the mouthpiece. It must remain closed whenever it is out of your mouth. If water gets into your breathing bag it will come into contact with the carbon dioxide absorbent and create a dangerous gas. This gas will kill you."

"Why are we using such dangerous equipment?"

"Don't you dumbbells listen? One, there are no bubbles - very little noise. It is very stealthy. Navy SEALS, Russian and Chinese special forces use oxygen re-breathers for sneak attacks."

"And the second reason?"

"You can stay submerged for four hours."

"Four hours. Shit, I'd look like a prune."

****

Djinni spent the next hour demonstrating how to fill the carbon dioxide absorbent canister, attach the oxygen bottle, and adjust the flow control valves. He then had everyone demonstrate opening and closing the mouthpiece valve before and after removing it from their mouth.

"One more thing. If you ever feel a twitch in your eyes or uncontrollable eye movement, you must surface immediately. Some people are more sensitive to pure oxygen than others. And if you've been drinking or doing drugs it's likely to be much worse. All right, everyone put on your equipment and let's get started. Khalid, you've used this gear before so buddy up with Hakeem. Ziad, you tag along with Hakeem and Khalid. Osaman, you dived this rig in the Caspian and Med, right?"

"Makhachkala and Libya."

"Good, your dive buddy is Ramin. Okay, everyone in the water. I'll hand over your propulsion unit when you're ready. Remember, thirty-three feet maximum."

"Come on, Ramin," said Osaman. "Let's beat these guys to the bottom."

"Stay clear of the kelp," shouted Djinni as Osaman and Ramin bit down on their mouthpieces and fell back into the ocean. While treading water, they cleared their facemasks and waited for Djinni to lower their propulsion units. Applying full power, Osaman and Ramin raced to the bottom as fast as their propulsion units would take them.

As they descended, they followed the trunk of a tall kelp tree. Once on the bottom, they made their way through the kelp forest. Here, they were joined by scores of bass, golden garibaldi, and a few small leopard sharks.

Each stalk of kelp anchored itself to the rocky bottom with a bundle of stiff roots. Looking up from the bottom, the divers could see long stalks reaching toward the surface, seeking nourishment from the sun. Once on the surface, the kelp stalks continued to grow, as much as two feet per day, gathering in large clusters spreading out hundreds of feet. In order to remain upright, hundreds of gas-filled, golf-ball-size pods grew along the length of each branch.

Once on the bottom, Osaman signaled for Ramin to follow

him toward a small opening between two stalks of kelp. Ramin followed Osaman through the dense stalks taking in the beauty and mystery of this underwater world. Mesmerized by the silence and fluid motion of brown stalks, Ramin began to feel more comfortable. His thoughts drifted to an imaginary underwater playground.

Suddenly, Ramin was hit in the fanny by a large animal. A burst of adrenaline raced up his spine as he considered the worst.

He had seen enough man-eating shark movies to know great white sharks killed humans - and they hunted in this part of the ocean. Terrified, he turned to face the monster - but there was nothing there but a forest of kelp trees and a few grazing fish.

Puzzled beyond words, he looked at his thigh. He was not cut or bleeding. He turned to find Osaman, but his dive partner had disappeared into an endless gallery of kelp. Confused and disoriented, he began to swim into what appeared to be a likely passage through the submerged forest. Mystified by the swaying kelp and diversity of life forms, he slowly regained his confidence.

Abruptly, he was rammed in the rear a second time - with more force than the first. Stunned and dumbfounded, he turned to see what sort of creature might be harassing him so brazenly. Behind a large kelp stalk, he saw the guilty prankster - a harbor seal. The spotted marine mammal blew a stream of bubbles and waved his flippers as an invitation to play a game of tag.

Beguiled by this amiable creature, Ramin swam toward the whiskered mammal, hoping it would remain long enough to be petted. The seal waited as Ramin approached, then, when they were only a few feet apart, turned and disappeared into the kelp forest.

Intent on retracing his path, Ramin looked back, hoping to find the route he thought he had taken. But there was no clear choice. Every stalk of kelp was more or less identical to all the others. Confused as to which direction he should take, he swam through a line of kelp that appeared to be familiar. But he soon changed his mind. He stopped and began to spin in circles, searching for the way out of the maze. He considered all his options - none of which were clear.

Where is Osaman? Where am I? He could feel his heart race - his breath quicken. He imagined the worst and began to panic. As he swam through the kelp, everything looked the same - nothing but long stalks of brown kelp - each one reaching out and grabbing his ankles like the tentacles of a huge octopus - choking tighter and tighter - strangling his legs and thighs - wrapping around his neck and arms.

He looked up with the notion to ascend, but the kelp was so thick it obscured the surface.

As he clawed his way through the twisting strands, pulling himself hand over hand along the rocky bottom, he tried to calm his thoughts, to maintain control over his reflexes and imaginings.

He suddenly realized both hands were bleeding - impaled by a fistful of sea urchin spines buried deep in his flesh. Looking down, he saw dozens of thorns protruding from his thighs and knees. In his confusion, he had accidentally crawled into a colony of these thorny bottom-dwellers.

There seemed to be no end in sight - no way up to the surface. The kelp blocked out the sun. All the radiance and colors of the seabed segued to a grayish panorama.

With blood oozing from his hands and legs, he pictured a great white shark stalking him - smelling his wounds - closing in for the kill. A lump of terror rose up in his throat.

His head began to spin - he didn't know up from down - his eyes twitched uncontrollably - pupils rolled back.

And then there was nothing.

THE SCARAB

Greg answered his phone on the second ring tone. "Hello, this is Greg."

"Greg. It's George. Detective Layton. How are you doin, you old frog?"

"Hey, Geo. My brother. Good to hear from you. You still chasing bad guys?"

"Oh, yeah. Quit drinking too. Lost forty pounds and feel like a kid again."

"I'm proud of you. What can I do for you?"

"Well, some SEALs on a training dive found this body tangled up in the kelp off Point Loma. He was wearing a Russian IDA-71 oxygen re-breather. They also found one of those underwater scooters nearby - Scuba Spyder. I think that was the name."

"That re-breather is a Cold War era rig. The Russkies used it back in the eighties. How deep was the dead diver?"

"Ninety feet. You and I both know that's too deep for oxygen."

"Jesus Christ. I guess he wanted to die with the fishes."

"Our victim is an Iraqi, mid-twenties, slender build. The only identifying mark was a small tattoo of a beetle on his right shoulder blade. We ran his prints. His name is Ramin Rubuka. His last residence before coming to the States was Saudi Arabia. He possessed a student visa and was enrolled at UC

Berkeley - engineering student. He has a younger brother, a recent graduate of Berkeley in nuclear physics. We found their address, an apartment in Berkeley, but the brothers have not been seen at school or at their apartment for several weeks. We ran them both through the NSA terrorist database. Both men are on the watch list."

"Scarab beetles. They represent the Egyptian goddess Isis. These tattoos are popular with ISIS terrorists and their followers. Whacked-out Hollywood entertainers get them too, as some sort of a status symbol. Some women have it tattooed on their boobs. Looks trashy to me, but what the hell do I know. I'm from the old school."

"Jeez, I'd like to feast my eyes on those pups."

"George, you may have quit drinking, but you haven't changed a bit. I mean that as a compliment. So other than to chat about old times or getting together at the next SEAL reunion, why are you calling me?"

"As I mentioned, this dead ISIS guy found off the coast, he's on the NSA terrorist watch list. What the hell was he doing out in the kelp with a Russian re-breather?"

"If I had to venture a guess, I'd say he was on a training dive."

"Training for what? That is the big question."

"Geo, do you know how many high-value targets are nearby? I'll give you a hint. Nuclear submarines - lots of them moored at Point Loma. And a couple of nuclear aircraft carriers, like the Ronald Reagan and Gerald Ford."

"I thought the Navy had good harbor security - hydrophones, combat swimmer barriers, and security dolphins. Remember when you and I did those practice sneak attacks? We embarrassed a lot of skippers when we popped a flare at their stern and they were obliged to serve us a big dish of ice cream in the officer's mess - for sinking their ship," said George.

"Yeah, those were the good old days. But that Emerson re-breather - that rig was deadly. We lost six teammates before the Navy switched to the Draeger. You and I, we were lucky, we never got caught."

George let loose with his rant. "Jesus, Greg. When will our leaders get the big picture? Our country is under attack by terrorists - mostly radical Islamic jihadists. Their infiltration is like a Trojan horse. Christ Almighty. We let them into our country without any vetting or documentation. Many of them are radicalized teens who have pledged their allegiance to ISIS and jihad. They reproduce like rabbits, three times faster than Americans. We don't know if they're murderers, rapists, or beheading fanatics. Most refugees don't even have a birth certificate. I feel compassion for their plight, but our immigration agents have no way to determine their intentions. Just look at what's going on in the EU. Terrorists raising hell all over - blowing up theaters, sports stadiums, and churches. These terrorists want to die a martyr so they blow themselves up or run around with a machete randomly chopping people, knowing they'll be shot dead - suicide by cop. That's why I called you, Greg. You know all about these things, and from what I've read, DARPA is playing a greater role in anti-terrorist operations. Anyway, you've got a much louder voice than I do. I'm just an old frog and burned-out Homicide Detective."

"Where does the Coronado PD fit into this?"

"My LT said it was none of our business - it was an accident. I'm just letting you know because it needs someone like you to get the right people involved."

"Thanks for calling. Let me make a few calls and I'll get back to you."

Greg had just hung up his phone when it rang again.

"Hello, Greg. It's David. I've called for a strategy meeting at our San Diego office for tomorrow, two in the afternoon. I've invited several key players, SPECWAR, Pentagon, DHS, NSA and FBI. Some SEALs found a dead diver wearing Russian oxygen gear tangled up in the kelp beds off Point Loma. We may be dealing with a possible ISIS attack. That's all I can say now. You need to be there."

"I'll catch the red eye. See you tomorrow."

****

"April, I'm home. Sorry to be late, but I got calls from George Layton and David." Greg wiggled his nose and raised his brows. "Something smells good. Ah, your famous spaghetti."

"David. Oh, that David. What's up?"

"They need me in San Diego tomorrow afternoon. I'm leaving on the red eye. It's an interesting case - possibly ISIS. Navy SPECWAR, DHS, NSA, and FBI will certainly be involved and the nature of the problem will probably include our dolphins."

"Do you want me to mobilize a response team?"

"I'll let you know after my meeting. I've got a worrisome feeling about this one."

"What can you tell me?"

"They found a dead diver off the coast of Point Loma. He was wearing a Russian oxygen re-breather. There's only one reason for him to be wearing an old Russian re-breather."

"Underwater sneak attack!"

"You're one smart cookie."

"You got time for dinner?"

"Are you kidding? I love your world-famous spaghetti. Can we eat early? I need to catch the eight o'clock flight. It arrives in San Diego at one in the morning. That will give me time to prepare for our afternoon meeting."

REHEARSAL

"Your brother should have listened to me, Hakeem. His careless behavior cost him his life before he could fulfill his jihad and achieve martyrdom. He should have followed my instructions." Djinni maligned Hakeem while the three Chechens smirked. Hakeem bowed his head and said a silent prayer to Allah to give his brother the status of a martyr and bless him with a houri - a most beautiful virgin to take whenever he wished. As he prayed the Chechens snickered.

"Stop sobbing, you fucking crybaby," muttered Ziad. "We've got a job to do and you're part of the plan."

"Leave him alone. Get your gear and meet me at the boat," said Djinni. "We'll spend some time reviewing our dive plan before heading to the site."

There was no love lost between the Chets and Arabs. They shared little in the way of culture or motivations except for their reverence to Allah and jihad - the destruction of all infidels.

Djinni planned the rehearsal dive with the Ortega security force in mind. He already knew it would take about thirty minutes for the private security helicopter to arrive and issue their hollow warnings. Their threat to call the Coast Guard was nothing more than a veiled possibility. And even if the security police called the Coast Guard, the nearest responder was in Oceanside, an hour or more away.

"You should arrive at the target location in about ten minutes," Djinni had told them. "Five minutes to videotape the immediate area and another twenty-five minutes to return against the incoming force of the cooling water - forty minutes total."

"What about sea monsters - sharks, moray eels?" Hakeem was fearful of the unknown creatures that may lurk inside a long, dark pipeline. "I've been reading about the dangerous sea life in these waters. One story was about a giant grouper - six hundred pounds. He swallowed a diver up to his waist - dragged him by the head into deep water. And an electric ray they call Torpedo. They've killed divers with an electric shock. But according to the local fishermen, the nastiest creature of all is the Humboldt squid. The locals call them red devils. They're huge - up to a hundred pounds and have ten tentacles, each lined with suction cups surrounded by cat-like claws. These schools of cannibals are like piranhas - they attack in roaming packs. They'll strip the flesh off a diver in a matter of seconds with their large parrot-like beak," Hakeem breathlessly declared.

"Hakeem! Don't get yourself all worked up. Yeah, sharks bite people. Do you know of anyone being killed by a shark?"

"No, but I've read about it. I read about fishermen and divers being attacked and killed by Humboldt squid too."

"How about a giant grouper or electric ray? Do you know anyone who has even seen one?" Djinni was getting fed up with Hakeem's phobias.

"No, but... but..."

"Don't give me any of your but...but shit. You've got a mission to do. Deal with it," barked Djinni. "We'll depart from the Dana Point marina aboard *Lionfish* at midnight. It's a short run to the Ortega power plant. I have the GPS coordinates of the induction pipe entrance. Do exactly as I say and you'll live to see the death of the infidels. And if for some reason you sacrifice your life in the name of jihad, you will receive the seven blessings from Allah in the afterlife. That's everyone's goal - right?"

Everyone looked around for consensus and nodded.

"There's one more thing you need to know. The mouth of the pipeline is only a few feet from the La Jolla Trench. It's a massive underwater canyon - drops straight down to a thousand feet along a fault line. Don't swim near it - the current might carry you into the abyss." The men looked at each other, then back to Djinni not knowing if he was serious or joking.

"You're kidding, aren't you?" asked Osaman.

"No, I'm dead serious. You can't miss it. Even in the dark of the night, the trench is darker, and you can feel the current pulling you toward it."

In spite of their trepidation, the Chechens did their best to keep their cool. Hakeem's imagination kidnapped his courage, flooding his stomach with adrenaline. He began to vomit over the gunwale.

At precisely midnight, Djinni engaged *Lionfish* and motored slowly into the ship channel until she was clear of the no wake zone. The overcast sky and new moon proved to make this the darkest night of the month - the best possible cover. As soon as he crossed the tip of the Del Mar harbor breakwater, he pushed the throttle to the hilt.

"Suit up. We'll be there shortly."

****

"Divers in the water! The entrance to the induction pipeline is directly below you. My depth sounder reads thirty-five feet. Take your time - don't overwork your re-breathers. Let the propulsion units do the work. Ziad and Khalid, you go first. Osaman and Hakeem, you follow a couple of meters back."

With their mouthpieces gripped firmly between their teeth, Ziad and Khalid powered up their Scuba Spyder underwater propulsion units and dove toward the pipe entrance. Hakeem and Osaman followed a few feet behind.

As the men descended, Hakeem could feel the power of the current sucking him downward - triggering powerful thoughts of being trapped in this black tunnel or attacked by some unknown sea monster. He immediately tensed up and backed off the power to his scooter, but the force of the incoming water pulled him deeper into the interior. A low-frequency humming noise from the power plant tightened his senses. What if there were some sharks or giant squid living down here - or a man-eating grouper? The blackness would be a perfect hideout for a hungry beast. What if there were some other creatures - possibly mutations from nuclear radiation - Godzilla or some giant carnivore he had seen in the movies? His imagination ran amok and he began to shiver.

As his anxieties intensified, so did his uncontrollable shaking. Irrepressible panic overcame his senses. His respiratory rate increased, resulting in overworking his re-breather and causing his carbon dioxide level to climb to a dangerous, hallucinogenic state. His wild mental imagery began to overpower his common sense and cognitive thinking. He could no longer stand the terror gathering in his belly.

Osaman looked back at Hakeem and waved for him to catch up. He pointed his flashlight at the face of his dive buddy. Hakeem's eyes were rolled back, his body convulsing in fear. Osaman knew Hakeem's re-breather could not process the excess carbon dioxide from his hyperventilation and raced to his aid. Taking a firm grip on Hakeem's harness, he applied full power to his propulsion unit and pulled Hakeem back to the surface.

"Hakeem is out of it. He's claustrophobic. He'll never make it inside the pipe!" he shouted to Djinni.

"Son of a bitch. What a fucking mess. Help me get him into the boat."

Hakeem quickly regained some sense of reality. "I'm sorry. I can't do this. Please, Allah. Please, Djinni. Forgive me."

"We've got to get Hakeem into the cabin - keep him out of sight. Store the dive gear. Get dressed as a fisherman. The security police will be here soon."

"What about Ziad and Khalid?"

"They'd better be back soon. The security helicopter will arrive soon. As long as they don't come up while the helicopter is overhead we should be safe. Claustrophobia! Why didn't he tell me earlier?"

Twenty-two minutes later, Ziad and Khalid surfaced.

"Where have you been?" Djinni was livid.

"We swam up to the rotating biological intervention screen. Sure glad we don't have to cut through that contraption."

"Hurry up and get in the boat. Security will be here any minute," Djinni barked.

The divers clambered aboard and quickly stored their equipment below deck. Djinni started the engines and sped out of the restricted area.

"What's wrong with Hakeem?" asked Ziad.

"He's afraid of dark spaces. Froze up and went berserk."

"What are we going to do?"

"Plan B."

"What's plan B?"

"Fuck if I know," growled Djinni.

GRASPING FOR STRAWS

Sitting at one end of the long conference table, David Stratton, Executive Director of DARPA, called the meeting to order. Greg sat at the opposite end. On his left sat Admiral Dobbins, Chief SPECWAR; General Goodson, Pentagon, and Samuel (Sam) Broderick, Director of the Department of Homeland Security. To his right sat Edward (Eddie) Patton, Director of the Anti-Terrorist Division of the Federal Bureau of Investigation; Allan Rusk, Director West Coast DARPA Marine Mammal Center; Terry Stockman, Head of the National Security Agency; Gordon Paris, Chief Executive Officer of Bluestar Security Services, and Richard Winslow, Chief of Security, Ortega nuclear power plant.

"Gentlemen, thank you for joining us today. We've much to discuss. It appears we may have a major security breach at the Ortega nuclear power plant. This all began when a group of Navy SEALs found a body floating in the kelp bed off Point Loma. The diver was identified as Ramin Rubuka. He was wearing a Russian IDA-71 oxygen re-breather. Cause of death was oxygen poisoning. He had a small tattoo of a scarab beetle on his right shoulder blade. These are popular with ISIS operators. He has a younger brother, a nuclear physicist named Hakeem Rubuka. They both attend UC Berkeley. We ran them through the NSA and DHS watch lists. Both came back positive. That's all we know at this time."

"Goddamn it. Why are we allowing potential terrorists to attend the University of California?" shouted Eddie.

"Both have undergraduate degrees. Hakeem has a BS degree in nuclear physics. The dead brother earned one in engineering," said Sam, shaking his head. "It is quite amazing to me how quickly intelligent people can become radicalized. Maybe it is in their DNA."

"Taxpayers probably paid for their education." Hostile emotions seeped into the atmosphere.

"That's something to be concerned with, but let's continue with a briefing. Gordon, you're next."

"Thank you, David. I have two short videos to show you. The first was taken by security cameras from our helicopter over a period of several weeks." David pushed the play button.

"This video shows multiple incursions by a thirty-foot Grady-White named *Lionfish*. Each intrusion lasted approximately thirty to forty minutes. The skipper has not been identified but our facial recognition team is confident they will have an ID on him shortly. The next video shows the same vessel and skipper with another man on deck. They are both dressed like fishermen."

"Hold it right there!" Greg stood and walked up to the screen. "This character is wearing a black eye patch. That certainly narrows the field of suspects. When was this video taken?"

"0100 last Thursday. If you look closely, you can see an underwater flashlight and weight belt on the deck. While the skipper claimed to be fishing, we believe this is a dive boat. The boat is registered to Abdul al Mijou ibn Bagot. He is the son of Sheik Mijou Bagot, a wealthy Saudi oil baron sympathetic to the ISIS movement. Abdul also attends UC Berkeley on a student visa and is on the NSA watch list. He allegedly has a sizeable monthly allowance and is fond of white college women." Gordon powered off the video and returned to his chair.

"Goddamn! Why don't we bring the entire ISIS army to UC Berkeley? Give em all smartphones, a nice apartment, free education, free healthcare, maybe even a free trip to the Mustang Ranch whenever their pecker gets lonely. This absurdity has to cease." Admiral Dobbins pounded his fist on the table. Everyone looked around the room mumbling their agreement.

"We understand your frustration, Admiral. That's why we are here - to do something about it."

"Sorry, gentlemen. Let's move on."

"Our next speaker is Richard Winslow. He's the Chief of Security at the Ortega facility. Richard, you have the floor."

"Thank you, David. I too have a short video. This was also taken last Thursday morning at precisely one-forty. The video came from one of our pump room night vision cameras focused on the rotating biological intervention screen. There, you can see a flash of light - there again - another flash of light from inside the induction pipe. There are no marine animals that can make that much light, so it had to be a diver with an underwater flashlight."

"How in the hell did a diver get inside the induction pipe? Don't you have a steel security grill at the entrance?" asked Broderick.

"We've put them and they rust away within two years. Besides, anyone can cut through them with a hacksaw or explosive rebar cutter."

"Could you estimate the distance to the source of this light?" David asked.

"It could have been a reflection from someone several feet down the pipe. Hard to say. It may have been from a video camera - it was very intense."

The men glanced at the faces of their compatriots; each wore a disquieted expression.

"Whew! That's a disturbing set of data," said David, glancing around the table. "What is your assessment, Gordon?"

"This is a typical recon maneuver by ISIS. They always check out the security first, so I'm not surprised they repeatedly entered the restricted zone to test our policing practices. The divers were probably investigating how they might get past the rotating biological intervention screen and gain access to the cooling pumps."

"You mean they intend to blow up the cooling pumps? My God! That would be an unimaginable catastrophe," exclaimed Samuel.

"No shit!" quipped Terry.

"If Ortega melted down, it would be the worst disaster in the history of mankind. Unimaginable," professed Samuel. "Twenty, maybe thirty thousand deaths in the first days."

"Anyone got an idea of the long term radiation hazards?" asked David.

"You don't want to know," replied Samuel.

"Goddamn it, Sam. We all have a right to know the truth! Give us your best estimate."

"If there is a full meltdown, our world as we know it will end. Give it ten years and not one living creature will be alive within a hundred miles." Samuel's face quickly drained of color. The mere thought of this level of death and destruction brought tears to the corners of his eyes.

"This all fits with the dead diver," said David with a tone of immediacy. "We must find a way to stop them. Eddie, bring in the Coast Guard and Harbor Police. We need to know where this boat, *Lionfish*, is moored. It could be as far north as Dana Point or Oxnard. Let's get a team on that now. And keep working on the facial recognition for the one-eyed skipper. There can't be too many of them in the database. Your men need to grab this Abdul character and bring him in for questioning. I don't care what you have to do, drugs, mind reading, whatever it takes to get him to talk. Greg, you'd better get a team of dolphins in the water. We'll need them to patrol the red zone and the entrance to the cooling water induction pipe."

"We'll mobilize our most intelligent and experienced dolphin partners from the Cape as well as San Diego." Greg nodded in the direction of Allan Rusk. "Allan is also our EOD expert."

Allan nodded his appreciation for the compliment from his boss.

Greg continued. "Hopefully we can shut this potential terrorist threat down before it develops into something more sinister. I recommend we have two of our dolphins patrolling the restricted zone twenty-four-seven. What do you think, Allan? Your West Coast dolphins know this area."

"That's the best thing to do until we get more intel. If these terrorists plan to use explosives, then we'll bring in our EOD guys. Some of these saboteurs have more advanced explosive techniques. That's when it gets a bit dicey."

"Allan is our best man for any explosive ordnance disposal operation. He's been there, done that before. His dolphin teams have located, disarmed, or safely destroyed thousands of floating mines and underwater explosives in the Persian Gulf and other hot spots around the world." Greg took a deep breath and paused to let the urgency of the situation sink in.

Allan interjected, "Not to mention the unmentionable, but these courageous animals have also nullified fifty-two enemy diver saboteurs since nine-eleven." Allan interjected this morsel of "need to know" classified information to remind everyone that some dolphins had real combat experience.

Greg continued. "Thanks, Allan. All of our teams are trained in Dolphinese and *Songbook* communication protocols. And they will be ready to use deadly force if necessary. Is that right?"

"Absolutely."

The men looked around the room for any detractors. Seeing none, David stood to make his closing remarks.

"Let's keep this under wraps - top secret - no fucking media leaks. Got it! These magnanimous dolphins are our partners - they do this because they like it. Anyone who doubts this can ask them directly." Everyone chuckled at David's levity. "Greg, can you coordinate the deployment of our best assets on this operation. Spare nothing. Call me if you need anything."

"I'm on it."

"Listen, everyone. Keep Greg advised. He's the point man for this mission."

****

Greg left the meeting and immediately dialed April.

"Hi. It's me. How's my girl?"

"I miss you. When are you coming home?"

"Not soon enough."

"Why not? What's going on?"

"We need you and some of our dolphin teams in San Diego. Please mobilize Uno and Luke. West Coast DARPA people will handle all the logistics. Bring your *Songbook* hardware and the new dolphin underwater communication equipment too. Ask Chief Pace and Wagner to join you. We'll use some West Coast SEAL vet-techs and EOD personnel to support the operation."

"Sounds like a major expedition. Where are you staying?"

"The DARPA guest cottage."

"Wait, what about Adam. He's our patriarch and ambassador. The other dolphins look up to him for leadership."

"I thought he was happiest when he was with his new girlfriend in the conservatory."

"He cares for her very much. But he's also full of piss and vinegar."

"I suggest you have a one on one with him. Like all our missions, this one could be dangerous. But I agree Adam would make the team stronger."

"I'll talk to him today and leave it up to him. We'll fly out on the DARPA jet. We should be in San Diego by four. Love you."

"Love you too. See you tomorrow."

****

70

Dressed in a wetsuit top, April dove into the training tank. Adam was waiting for her. They met in the middle of the tank where April reached out and stroked the top of his head. When they were eye to eye, April began to speak into her DULAN comm. system.

[APRIL] Hello Adam. It is good to swim with you.

[ADAM] Hi April. We have not been in the water together for several months. You must be very busy. Or maybe you have something special to tell me.

[APRIL] How do you manage to read my mind?

[ADAM] It is the way of the dolphin. Like a game of chess. Our brain sees into the future and knows the past.

[APRIL] Greg has a dangerous mission in California. Uno and Luke are leaving tomorrow to join him. I'm going too. Would you like to lead the dolphin team?"

[ADAM] I would be happy to lead my dive buddies. What will we do?

[APRIL] We will find out later. What about Susy? She'll miss you very much.

[ADAM] Susy loves our life together. Susy will miss me and I will miss her. But this is our choice. We want to partner with humans. That is the best way for both species.

[APRIL] Yes. That is the best way. We will work and play and live our lives in harmony. Eve is no longer with us. You are the only ambassador dolphin.

April choked up from the memories she shared with Eve.

[ADAM] I understand your feelings. I feel them too. I miss Eve. She made me laugh.

Adam brushed his head against April's shoulder and let out a long trickle of tiny bubbles.

[APRIL] Say goodbye to Susy for me.

X-RAY

For the dolphins, a cross-country flight in their custom-built jumbo jet provided the same kind of thrill as a kid's first visit to the latest tourist attraction - Spaceland.

The spacious travel tanks provided ample room for a leisurely journey. They were equipped with a high-volume filtration system and filled with temperature-stabilized seawater.

From a dolphin's point of view, everything was first-class. The food was exceptional. Chasing live squid around their travel tank before gobbling them up with a quick nip was an entertaining and gratifying experience.

The occasional bumpy moments broke up the monotony and, as they did for humans, made a good story to tell their friends and families when they returned to the conservatory.

Greg arrived at the airport as their flight taxied up to the DARPA terminal at the North Island Naval Air Station.

"Hi there, handsome. Nice of you to meet us," said April as she took hold of Greg's hand and gave him a quick peck on the cheek.

"How was your flight? Any rough weather?"

"A bit bumpy over Texas. The dolphins loved it, especially Uno. He was disappointed when the weather cleared, and squealed for more. He'll calm down once he gets to meet his

West Coast counterparts. Then he'll whistle the time away with story after story of his first ever jumbo jet flight and the thrill of chasing live squid for dinner at 40,000 feet."

"Come with me. We have a meeting with Allan Rusk at the conservatory. We need his help developing a security plan including dolphin patrol schedules, rules of engagement, tactics. You know the drill."

Greg grabbed the big bags while April tossed her carry-on over her shoulder. During the short ride to the DARPA facility, Greg painted the overall picture - the dead diver, the Russian re-breather, the propulsion unit, the repeated incursions into the Ortega restricted zone, a one-eyed terrorist, and the pipeline video.

****

"Good afternoon, Greg. Nice to see you brought the better half. Good day to you, April." Allan smiled, shook hands with Greg and touched cheeks with April.

"Thanks for arranging this great San Diego weather. Brings back a lot of good memories. How's Felicia and the kids?"

"Doing great. She just returned from Seattle visiting her sister. I've been batching it. Naturally, I'm glad she's home. No more TV dinners. She's anxious to see you. I hope you're free this evening."

Greg and April had known Allan for several years from the time Greg was head of the DARPA Point Loma facility and April was a young naval officer. Greg had recruited Allan to be his Chief Veterinarian after he retired from a twenty-two-year naval career. His last assignment was head of the dolphin health and welfare operations at the Navy Marine Mammal Center.

Allan Rusk received a DVM specializing in cetaceans from UC Davis - the best vet university in the country. He later earned an MBA from Harvard.

He acquired a reputation as an imaginative, enthusiastic,

and trusting animal rights advocate. He was also widely regarded as a master practical joker. He seemed to always have a plastic spider or rubber snake handy and pulled off some truly memorable pranks.

Together, he and Felicia continued to invest much of their spare time promoting the United Nations Dolphin Equality Doctrine, often going up against some powerful and dangerous forces in their quest to protect cetaceans from death or injury due to reckless commercial fishing practices.

April turned to Greg. "Does that mean he's taking us out to dinner?"

Allan quickly replied, "It will be my pleasure. Besides, Felicia wants to know all about how you two got together. From what I know, it was love at first sight," Allan chuckled.

As they walked, Allan pointed out the key features of the new dolphin conservatory facility.

"This place is like an airport - we never stop expanding. We just finished enlarging the DSB docking facilities - got enough space for six of the new dolphin support boats and a couple of extra-large floating holding tanks." Allan pointed in the direction of the small harbor.

"How many of our aquatic friends do you have at the conservatory?" asked April.

"Ninety. Forty adult males, thirty-eight adult females - six are pregnant - and twelve juveniles."

"And how many are qualified in Dolphinese?"

"Roughly half the adults. Some learn faster than others, just like humans. However, generally speaking, they learn the basics twice as fast as we humans learn to speak English."

"Hey, I see you've got a helicopter. And she's rigged with dolphin water slides and quick-pick recovery cradles. That's a fantastic idea, Allan."

"Yeah, I thought you'd be impressed. Our dolphins love it. One second they're inside their holding tank - then, when they get the signal, the helicopter slows to twenty knots, their tank door drops open and they slide out head-first into the ocean. They truly enjoy jumping out of a helicopter and it's exciting for us to watch. Some of the SEAL vet-techs have done it too - mostly for bragging rights."

"I'd like to see that while we're here. Most of our work is ASW-related, but if it works for you, it'll work for us."

"We can thank our friends in congress. DARPA HQ continues to get the money we've requested for new facilities, training equipment, computers, IT engineers, linguists. You ask for it, they'll get it. The conservatory is fabulous, but we get more involved in special ops every month. In addition to our West Coast dolphin conservatory, there are five SEAL teams and three EOD platoons stationed on this base. And even though half of them are deployed somewhere around the globe, this place is one giant beehive - eighty acres and over two billion dollars of Hooyah!"

April gazed out the picture window at a company of BUD/S trainees trudging along the soft sand toward Coronado - torment painted across each sweaty face. A "rabbit" instructor ran alongside the group disparaging the slowpokes one minute - rallying them the next. April looked at Greg and chuckled. "With so much testosterone, there must be some rocking good nightlife in these parts."

"I wouldn't know," Allan replied cryptically.

"Let's get some coffee and have a talk. I've got some intriguing information to share with you. Follow me to the conference room." Allan led Greg and April to the conference room where they each poured a mug of coffee and took a seat.

Allan began. "I've been doing some research on the Ortega nuclear power plant and discovered some interesting facts. First, the Nuclear Regulatory Commission ordered them to shut the place down several years ago. This is a twenty-year, one hundred billion-dollar project. The owners are balking - taking short cuts - missing deadlines. Over the past few years, they've been cited by the NRC for several infractions - mostly safety issues - carelessness and security violations. They had one incident of sabotage - someone on the inside put seawater in the fuel tank of a backup generator. The generator was knocked out of commission. If there had been a real emergency, there would be no power to run the water pumps."

"Jesus, that's pretty much what happened at Fukushima."

"They've also been found guilty of intimidation - threatening whistleblowers - anyone they believe might go public with knowledge of security or safety infractions."

"Where'd you find all this information?" April asked.

"The Internet mostly. I had to do a little detective work, but it's all there in black and white. Some of the NRC information was posted on their web site; the rest was in the daily news. But the real gem came from a report written by a consultant, Doctor Benjamin DeNieto. He's a highly respected nuclear physicist and former professor. He was retained by NRC and Ortega Power to advise them of potential radioactive malevolence - *before the Ortega plant was built*."

"Goddamn. So the power company knew about the potential for a terrorist attack and did nothing about it?" April shook her head in condemnation.

"Yup. And it gets worse. Can you guess the top two targets cited in Doctor DeNieto's report?" Allan raised his eyebrows, and then scanned the faces of his guests.

"Oh, hell, I'm just guessing. The cooling pumps?"

"Good thinking, April. What was the second most likely terrorist target?"

"Give me a second." April placed her index finger against her temple. "Nuclear waste storage."

"Damn, it's sure gratifying to work with such brilliant people."

Allan's appreciation for April's responses quickly gave way to frustration. "Most people think of a power plant as improving the quality of life. A few folks know the real dangers. A handful of activists try to do something about it, including my wife. She's interested in radiation effects on marine life. The bottom line is profit. There's only one motive - money - pure avarice. They, and I mean the owners, politicians, and regulators, are all in the game. They don't give one hoot about the health and safety of their customers or the debilitating effects on the local marine biomass. If they did, they'd never have built this nuclear power plant on one of the most beautiful beaches in the world - and never on a major seismic fault. Can you believe it?"

Greg considered the environmental factors for a few seconds and then replied, "Yeah, I recall the sales pitch for nuclear. Unlimited, low-cost energy for everyone. Clean, safe electricity. No worries about blackouts. No need to be concerned about air pollution from coal or fossil fuels. And definitely no worries about radiation in the air or in the ocean. The people will be overjoyed and every fish in the sea will be happy."

April cringed at the thought of another Fukushima - on the shores of southern California.

Allan picked up the pace of their reckless contempt for proper safety procedures. "They've even modified the canisters for storing nuclear waste to save money by reducing the thickness of the steel. Moreover, they're using cheap stainless steel that is subject to cracking by way of chlorine-induced stress corrosion from salt water mist. I could go on and on. It makes me furious." Bubbles of scornful perspiration blossomed from Allan's forehead.

"They've got no place to put them - these canisters. Each one is a potential dirty bomb containing more deadly radiation than Chernobyl. And Ortega has fifty of them." Allan was agitated by the state of affairs. "We read and hear about these potential hazards almost weekly. The politicians call the activists conspiracy theorists. There are lots of hollow promises but no action." Allan grimaced and shook his head. "Did you know there are over a hundred nuclear power plants in the United States?

They all share the same problem."

"Where are they going to store their nuclear waste?" asked April.

"You won't believe it. The federal government promised to store our nation's nuclear waste in Nevada, but the deal fell apart. There are over a hundred nuclear power reactors in America and all have the same problem - no place to store the nuclear waste. Ortega plans to store their nuclear waste canisters next to the plant - *on the fucking beach!*" Allan didn't often use the F-bomb, but when he did, it was usually spontaneous, explosive, and provocative.

"That is very fucking disturbing." April had no qualms about equating her feelings with her compatriots. Greg chuckled at her cheeky candor.

"You know, these terrorists get most of their information from the Internet?" Greg jumped back into the dialog. "They don't need spies or moles. Everything they need is public information - blueprints, design specifications, cooling water plumbing schematics, safety, and security, everything you ever wanted to know about the Ortega plant is available on the Internet. How stupid is that? A ten-year-old could figure it out." As usual, Greg had also done his homework.

"You're right. It's been well documented in the court proceedings. The NRC continues to assess millions of dollars in fines against these renegade plants. Nothing seems to work. The power company says it's not their problem."

"Let's take a break. Come on, Allan, show April and me this fabulous new conservatory of yours. What's new with your Pacific bottlenose dolphins?"

"I'm so glad you asked. I've got a surprise in store for you both." Allan gave Greg the smile of a friendly competitor. "You know we don't make too many breakthroughs around here. Besides, it's damn hard to beat that chess game demonstration you sponsored. Uno put a real hurt on Mr. Kasorovski. However, we occasionally find a way to upstage you East Coast rascals. And when we do, it's usually monumental. You and your team of researchers are used to getting all the glory. Now it's our turn. We have one very special dolphin. His name is Ray. The EOD guys nicknamed him X-ray because… well, come with me and I'll show you."

Allan led April and Greg down the hall through the security doors to the dolphin training tank.

"Have a seat next to me at the control console and watch the monitor. I'm going to play a videotape of an experiment we did last week with X-ray."

Greg and April sat facing the large high-resolution flat panel monitor while Allan booted up the video.

"Okay, it's ready to go. But first I'll set the stage. Our EOD team fashioned a make-believe IED using a nine-volt battery, a cheap cell phone, and a standard detonator circuit. After assembly, the device was packaged inside a waterproof aluminum container about the size of a cigar box. Watch the monitor and read the dialog. You're in for one big surprise."

[ALLAN] Hello X-ray. How are you today?

[X-RAY] Awesome. And how are you?

[ALLAN] I am very good. Thank you for asking. Do you see the box in the center of the tank?

[X-RAY] Yes. I see it.

[ALLAN] What is the box material?

X-ray swam to the box and circled it several times with his rostrum rubbing against the container.

[X-RAY] Aluminum. The box is aluminum.

The text on the monitor scrolled down line by line as the conversation continued.

[ALLAN] Very good. Tell me what is inside the box?

April look at Greg and mumbled, "This is getting interesting."

X-ray placed his rostrum at the top of the box, then slowly moved his head from side to side, systematically working his rostrum to the bottom of the box in a raster scan pattern.

[X-RAY] I have an image of the contents of the box. I do not know how to describe it in words. I will send you the image. Give me a moment to gather the data.

Several seconds later, an image slowly appeared, one line of pixels at a time.

[X-RAY]

"Oh, my God!" Greg cried out raising both hands above his head like a soccer player after scoring the winning goal at the World Cup Championships.

"No, this cannot be!" April jerked back and gasped. "Come on, Allan. You've got to be kidding. This must be a trick."

"Nope, I swear to God, stick a hundred needles in my eye if I tell a lie. X-ray did this. This is a recorded transmission in real time. He's well versed in *Songbook* protocols and Dolphinese communication. This is a huge amount of data. It's just a black and white image, but our guys went berserk when they saw it."

"Christ, you can see the battery, the wires, cell phone. This is incredible. I'm blown away. April, can you believe this?"

"It's incomprehensible - hard to believe it's real. I don't understand how X-ray is able to transmit this much data. Give me a moment to digest this. This is so awesome. What an accomplishment. Allan, you and your team should be very proud. How big is this image file?"

"Almost fifty kilobytes."

"Unbelievable. How do you think he does it?"

"We're still trying to figure that out. Probably some sort of natural frequency response or soft X-rays combined with Doppler effects. X-ray must be capable of emitting much higher frequencies than previously believed possible."

"I'm truly flabbergasted. What an incredible discovery. The scientific community won't buy it. They're still in lockstep with their narcissistic folly and hubris." Greg held a marveled expression.

"I didn't plan on submitting a scientific paper for peer review. It's classified top secret and will remain that way for some time."

"Who else has seen this?" asked Greg.

"The three of us, two of our senior researchers, and our senior EOD man, Warrant Officer Cliff Brady. Everyone has a top secret clearance."

"I assume everything is documented, encrypted and secure."

"Oh, yeah. By the book."

WILLY'S ON THE COVE

"Where's Allan taking us to dinner?" asked April as she stepped from the shower and began to dry off her hair.

"Willy's on the Cove. It's in La Jolla overlooking the ocean. You've been there before."

"Yeah, once, a long time ago when I was in the Navy. Golly, that seems like yesterday, but it's been six years."

"What do you want to eat for dinner?"

"Chilean sea bass is my favorite. How about you?"

"Langostinos a la Ensenada." We can't get them on the East Coast. The last time I had them was in Baja, years ago. Tiny little critters, but oh, so delicious with mango salsa and mild chili's."

"And dessert. What's your pleasure?" April dropped her towel and faced Greg, beads of water clinging to her naked flesh.

"Oh, my. April, you are so beautiful." Greg wrapped his arm around her waist pulling her closer.

"Hey, now your shirt is all wet."

Greg looked down at two wet circles.

"Oops. No worries, sweetie. It's just water."

April wrapped her arms around his torso and buried her wet head against his shoulder.

"I love you so much." She traced her wet tongue across his ear.

"What's on the menu?"

"Just about everything you could ever want." She grasped his buttocks pulling him closer, then gave him a warm, wet kiss on the lips. "We've got plenty of time to..."

The chimes of Greg's smartphone broke up their coquetry. April drew back with a frivolous pout.

Greg put his libidinous thoughts in neutral and answered his phone while April walked over to the closet to select her evening attire.

"Hello, Eddie. What's up?"

"I've got some interesting news. You got a minute?"

"Yeah. Sure. Go ahead."

"I've got an update on this Abdul character. He's dead - overdosed on some designer drug."

"Sorry to hear that. We needed a lead. How about the boat skipper? Any progress on his facial recognition?"

"Still working on it. *Lionfish* was recently sold to a San Diego investment banker. He's clean."

"You should have your forensic folks examine that Grady-White ASAP. There may be some DNA floating around - an old beer can, coffee cup, anything, even garbage."

"I'll get right on it."

"Our man may have bought another boat. See if you can find any recent sales from San Diego to LA. Same kind of boat - similar size and engines. Try Grady-White dealers first, then Sea Ray. Make sure you show them a digitally rendered composite picture with the eye patch. Also, check with the Zodiac dealers. They may be downsizing to an inflatable for stealth."

"Will do. Oh, yeah. One more thing, we got a call from a man named Dick Evans. He owns a dive shop in Mission Beach. He learned of the dead diver on the news. He said he thinks he sold a propulsion system to the dead guy. He told us there were six men in the group - one seemed to be the leader. He had a black patch over one eye."

"Holy shit! That's our man."

"I agree. The divers were recently certified. This guy Evans, he trained them to run the underwater scooters at La Jolla Shores."

"Did he give you a description of these divers?"

"He said they all spoke English with him but they talked to each other in a foreign language. The divers appeared to be twenty to thirty years of age. They ranged in height and weight but mostly modest build, five foot eight, give or take, and a hundred and thirty to a hundred and fifty pounds. Interestingly, they were all clean shaven. The leader was a little taller and looked to be sixty or older. He said the guy acted strange - almost like a cyborg."

"He's probably the leader of a terrorist cell - gets his funding and mission assignments from ISIS. Those divers are his jihadist toadies. They probably shaved their beards to make a good seal on their facemasks."

"He paid for all the gear in cash. Oh, and the divers all had the same tattoo on their right shoulder. It looked like some kind of a bug."

"It's called a scarab - considered divine by ancient Egyptians. ISIS followers think it is a mark of obedience to Allah and their ticket to martyrdom."

"I'll keep digging. Talk to you later."

Greg turned to April. "Well, Mr. One-eye is our man. Damn, NSA should have a full profile on this guy."

"Maybe the patch is a disguise?"

"April, my dear. You are so... beautiful... and illuminating. Why didn't I think of that?"

"What do you want me to wear to dinner - black or red?"

"Red is a little too campy. Better stick with the black. It's classy and will go great with those strappy high heels."

"Hedonist," April teased. "You'd better save room for my dessert."

****

Greg tossed the car keys to the valet while April took his arm and sashayed up the tile stairs to the main entrance.

"There they are." Allan stood and waved to Greg and April.

"Hi, sorry we're late. Got a call from Eddie. He had some interesting news, but it'll wait. Hello, Felicia. I believe we met a couple of times when I was living in San Diego."

"Nice to see you again. You haven't changed a bit. And you must be April. I've heard so many nice things about you. I'm delighted you could join us. What a beautiful dress."

"Thank you, Felicia. It's a pleasure to finally meet you too. I understand you're a strong advocate for dolphin rights. That must be a demanding challenge."

"To say the least. But let's not talk shop. Come. Sit. Order a drink. I want to hear all about you and how you and Greg hooked up. You're one lucky lady."

"What are you guys drinking?" asked Allan.

Looking at April, Greg replied, "Chardonnay, Coastal Prince if they have it."

"That's our favorite too." Allan caught the eye of the waiter. "A bottle of Coastal Prince Chardonnay. And put another bottle on ice, thank you."

"What a fabulous view - the moon reflecting across the sea - waves crashing against the cliff. This place is so… energizing." April was drawn to the tranquil splendor of the seascape.

"Look - there on the rocks - seals - two of them, sleeping." Felicia pointed out the window.

"This place is home to several colonies of seals, sea lions, harbor seals. They've got plenty of squid, sardines, anchovies, and greenback herring to eat."

"May I take your orders?" asked the waiter, cheerfully

grinning at April.

"Chilean sea bass with asparagus. Small Caesar salad - no croutons, please."

"And you, madam?"

Felicia pointed to the house special. "Lobster thermidor. Mixed fruit salad, please."

"And you, sir?"

"I'll have the Langostinos a la Ensenada, mild chili medley, and a Caesar salad," replied Greg.

The waiter focused his attention on Allan.

"I'll have a kosher hot dog with sweet relish and mustard in a paper basket."

Everyone was momentarily shocked. The waiter's expression was priceless. Felicia quickly responded, "Oh, Allan. Don't do that. It's embarrassing. He's up to his same old tricks."

April covered her laughter with her napkin. Greg smiled and shook his head while thinking back to similar moments of levity when he and Allan were single.

"Sorry. I'll have the filet, medium-rare with béarnaise sauce. Let's have the mixed oyster plate for starters."

"Thank you. The oyster plate will be right out," said the waiter.

"So, April, where and how did you and Greg meet? It must have been a storybook romance," asked Felicia.

Greg smiled and gave April a reassuring look. It was immediately apparent he enjoyed listening to April tell the story of their love affair as much as she took pleasure in telling it.

"Storybook romance?" April's eyes lit up as she reached for Greg's hand. "Yes, I guess you could call it that. I was fresh out of Annapolis, seeking adventure and a naval career. I was stationed at the Navy Marine Mammal Center in Point Loma. Our base was next to the old DARPA facility. That's where Greg worked. He was the director of the *Songbook* dolphin communication project - top secret stuff in those days. Anyway, one day my boss asked me if I'd like to take a temporary additional duty assignment to help Greg transfer the *Songbook* technology to the Navy. I was delighted to take on that assignment and, a few months later, Greg asked me to teach naval officers how to use *Songbook* protocols."

"That must have been very exciting - working on a leading edge program? I can easily understand how you may have been attracted to Greg." Felicia gave Greg a mischievous grin.

"It was much more than the tingle of romance. Greg actually wanted my help - my ideas regarding dolphin rights, the conservatory, and freedom of choice between a life in the conservatory or in the wild ocean."

"No wonder you fell for him."

"Oh, yeah. I was a goner right from the beginning." April giggled as she moved her hand up Greg's arm. "Well, a few months later Greg asked me to join his team working on the new DARPA dolphin conservatory in Cape Canaveral. That's where we connected - if you know what I mean?"

Felicia rolled her eyes. "Wow! Fireworks. So dreamy."

"Our first date was in a restaurant similar to this - on the beach - great atmosphere. Greg wore his customary khaki slacks, a colorful Bermuda print shirt, and dark blue deck shoes. The combination suited him well, especially with his gold Rolex Submariner. We ordered Chardonnay and the house specialty - stone crab." April took a deep breath and sighed. "That's it. It was the stone crab. Something in that critter made me fall head over heels for this handsome man." April leaned in and gave Greg a kiss on the cheek.

"That's a wonderful story. I fell for Allan in a similar way but it was not stone crab. I'm a bit embarrassed, but as a matter of fact, we met on a grunion hunt. They're not as tasty or romantic as stone crab."

"A grunion hunt? What the heck is a grunion?"

"It's a small fish that swims onto our Southern California beaches to spawn. They come ashore at night, by the thousands, once or twice a year. You don't need a fishing license to catch them - you can only use your hands. It's quite comical to see hundreds of men, women, and children chasing a squiggling fish only four inches long. Allan and I had a great time - we felt like teenagers. We've been married now for almost twenty years. Right, dear?"

"Twenty of the best years of my life."

Everyone cheered.

Allan raised his glass. "Long live the stone crabs and grunion." The foursome touched wine glasses.

"Well, it almost didn't have a happy ending," April continued. "The Navy transferred me to the Pentagon. I knew Greg loved me and I felt the same, so I had to make a big decision."

"And that was…" Felicia moved closer to hear April's reply.

"I resigned my commission and we were married. Our wedding day was the happiest day of my life. We're celebrating our anniversary next month."

****

"That was a terrific dinner. Did you enjoy yourself?" Greg asked as they waited for the valet to deliver their rental car.

"The company, food, and atmosphere - everything was fabulous. I enjoyed talking with Felicia too. She's got some interesting thoughts on dolphin conservation. She thinks we should use our dolphins as coastal messengers - harbingers spreading the word to wild dolphins about dangerous migration routes. She believes we should warn them about treacherous places - places like Taiji where the fishermen actively hunt for dolphins, eat them, and sell them to tourist attractions."

"That's an incredible concept."

"I thought so too." April snuggled up to Greg as they drove along the Silver Strand to the DARPA facility.

"Look at all those sailboats moored in the bay. I wonder what the people inside are doing on such a beautiful evening?"

She kissed Greg on the cheek. "How about you? Did you have a fun time?"

"It was excellent. Good to be with old friends."

"I hope you saved some room for my dessert."

PLAN B

"Hakeem!" Djinni shouted into the telephone. "What the fuck is this claustrophobia bullshit - your fear of enclosed spaces?"

"I can't help it if I feel trapped. I'm sorry. I can't control the feeling."

"Listen, I know how much you want to fulfill your promise to Allah and I have an idea that is worthy of your jihad and sacrifice. Meet me at the coffee house in an hour."

"Okay. Please don't be angry at me. I'll do anything to please Allah. I'll see you there." Hakeem felt a surge of atonement race through his chest. He muttered, "I wonder what Allah wants of me? Avenge my father - my brother - mother and sister?"

****

"Come in and take a seat. Do you want a coffee?" Djinni seemed uneasy.

"Sure. Thanks." Hakeem fidgeted in his uncomfortable wooden chair.

Djinni filled two cups of black coffee and joined Hakeem. Leaning closer, he let his eye scan across Hakeem's face, then smiled and touched his arm.

"Do you know why Sheik Mijou al Bogot wanted you and your brother to get technical degrees - you in nuclear physics,

Ramin in electrical engineering? Do you have any idea why he would pay your tuition and living expenses for five years while you attended Berkeley?"

"Ramin and I talked about it - his generosity. Our father died trying to repay him. We thought it was his way of paying his respects to our family and for us to keep an eye out for his son, Abdul."

"Well, that may have been part of his thinking. But the real reason was this mission. He saw what happened in Japan with the Fukushima meltdown. He believed he could duplicate that disaster on the infidels if he had the right people. He's been planning this mission for many years. He believed it was essential to have jihadists he could trust become educated in the science and technology of nuclear power in order to contribute their ideas to fulfill his mission. You and your brother were his chosen ones."

"Allahu Akbar. Praise be to Allah and the Sheik. I am sorry Ramin was unable to fulfill his obligation to the Sheik. What can I do to please my masters?"

"Allah has planted a seed in my head. A seed that only you can germinate."

"I don't understand. What is it Allah wishes me to do?"

"There are five million pounds of radioactive waste stored in steel canisters next to the Ortega power plant. These canisters contain deadly radioactive material with a half-life of tens of thousands of years. Americans call them dirty bombs."

"I know all about dry storage and isotope half-life. But what is my mission - how will I earn my seven blessings?"

"The storage canisters are manufactured using stainless-steel sheet metal, two millimeters thick. This is typical American cost cutting mentality - might as well put this radioactive scrap in a beer can. They bury the canisters along the shoreline a hundred feet from the high water line. Each canister contains the same amount of radioactive material released in the Chernobyl meltdown. If you can cause a leak - even a small one - in one of these canisters, it would be the biggest dirty bomb ever. Thousands would die and millions would have to leave the contaminated area - maybe twenty miles in diameter, depending on the wind. This is your mission - your ticket to sensual paradise and Allah's seven promises."

"Allahu Akbar. Thank you, Allah. And thank you, Djinni. How will I carry out this jihad?"

"You're going to place armor-piercing shaped charges onto the top of the dry storage canisters."

"I don't understand. I'm only familiar with IEDs made from heavy artillery shells. They're way too heavy. And besides, there are armed guards and a thirty-foot wall. How am I supposed to carry out my mission?"

"A drone, Hakeem. A small, remotely controlled drone."

"How can a small drone carry a heavy IED?"

"You don't understand the principles of shape charges. First, they are nothing like your typical IED. In fact, they don't even require a heavy charge to be effective. My shaped charges can penetrate steel to a depth of fifteen centimeters. These devices do not depend on melting the metal. It drills a hole using the kinetic energy from ultra-fast acceleration and the velocity of the wave front at the point of impact."

"How fast is that?"

"Thirty-five thousand feet per second - six miles per second."

Hakeem quickly did the conversion in his head.

"Yeek! Twenty-five million Gs. It's hard to fathom that much energy in such a short period of time." Hakeem gasped as he wrapped his mind around the physics.

"Allah has blessed us with a most powerful weapon." Djinni played into Hakeem's dream of martyrdom. "The power of this device will create a massive leak of deadly radiation into the atmosphere. There is no way to stop it."

"I had no idea how these things worked. How big is it?"

"About the size of a beer can - seven centimeters in

diameter, sixteen centimeters long, and half a kilo in weight. There is a contact switch attached to each of the landing pads. The timer starts when the drone lands on the lid. You can set the timer from five seconds to twenty-four hours. Then - kaboom - deadly radiation will begin to spew into the air."

"The mother of all dirty bombs." Hakeem was overjoyed. "Will I die a martyr?"

"Yes. Allah will bless you forever. You will have earned his highest praise - seven promises and endless sensual pleasure. Now let's head to the local hobby shop. We've got to buy a drone and you've got to learn how to fly it."

****

After scanning the display case containing several FAA approved drones, Djinni approached the clerk.

"Hi, my name is Vince. How can I help?"

"I'm looking for a video drone capable of carrying a two-pound payload."

"Follow me, sir. I've got the perfect solution. It's the same model that real estate agents use. The video is transmitted to a small LED monitor built into the control console. You can clearly see where you're heading and zoom in and out as needed. The USB flash drive can store thirty minutes of video. This baby has an FAA rating to five hundred feet and a range of a thousand yards. The quad battery-powered motors make it easy to fly and the built-in GPS allows you to program up to twenty data points. Come with me to the parking lot. I'll show you how simple it is. Chucky, watch the store, will ya. I'm going to demo this QuadViewer."

"Okay," replied Chucky.

Djinni and Hakeem followed Vince to the parking lot.

"I've flown this demo unit four times today. It's easy once you get the hang of it. You just look at the video display and fly wherever you wish. The rangefinder will signal when you are within a hundred feet of the flight envelope."

Vince placed the drone on the asphalt next to a handicapped parking slot. "This here button turns on the power. This dial shows the remaining battery life in minutes. You'll get about twenty minutes on a full charge. This is your joystick." Vince placed his index finger on each item as he talked. "This is your power and this red button is your auxiliary output. Pressing it will allow you to drop a small package on someone's front porch. Okay, understand?"

"How do I take off and land?"

"Push the power to twelve hundred rpm and she'll climb - add a bit more power if you want to go higher or are carrying extra weight. This little bumblebee will do exactly what you tell it. For landing, just reduce the power and pick a safe place to land. Press the home button and she'll automatically come back to where she took off. This baby can land on the palm of your hand. Pretty nifty, eh?"

"This thing is awesome," Hakeem was enthralled. "Can I give it a try?"

"Sure." Vince handed Hakeem the controller. "Just follow my instructions."

"Let's go."

"Turn the power on and power up to twelve hundred rpm. Then pull back on the joystick and slowly increase power to fifteen hundred rpm and climb to fifty feet - then level off and fly. Be careful maneuvering around light poles and tall trees. It's important to keep the drone in sight at all times. There are running lights for night flying."

Hakeem did exactly as he was told and to his delight, the drone lifted off the ground and climbed above the nearby light poles. He flew around the perimeter of the parking lot, dodging thirty-foot light poles, swooping to within inches above parked cars, climbing and descending while viewing the action on his monitor.

"We'll take it," said Djinni. "Do we need spare batteries?"

"It comes with a rechargeable battery that takes about an

hour to recharge or you can buy a couple of spares and swap them out as needed."

"Yeah, throw in a couple of spares. How much do I owe you?"

"Let's go inside and I'll ring you up."

Vince packed the drone, controller, camera, accessories, and spare batteries in the custom carrying case and rang up the total.

"That will be $832.55. Cash or charge?"

"Cash."

****

As they headed back to the car, Djinni asked. "How do you like your new toy? It's your passport to sensual paradise. Allah has made you seven promises. Now you have to prove you are worthy of his generosity."

"I am ready but perplexed. What exactly must I do? What is the plan?"

"We're going to check out our transportation and insertion point. Come, get in my truck. I'll take you there."

Djinni entered the Interstate and traveled south to the Tamarack exit, following the signs to Agua Hedionda lagoon. He pulled into the parking lot at the water sports outlet. Outside, on the grassy frontage, a line of ocean kayaks greeted the visitors. The salesman saw them before they saw him.

"Howdy, folks. Rick here. I've got the perfect kayak for the two of you." Djinni took an immediate interest.

"These are the best self-bailing ocean-going kayaks on the market. They're perfect for ocean paddling, fishing, or diving. They come in one- and two-man models. The wide beam makes them ideal for carrying extra gear - up to three hundred pounds."

"Do they come with an electric motor and transom?"

"You betcha. A two-horse MaxiTorque outboard, battery, and transom - a package deal. This here tandem fifteen footer will cruise forty miles on a single charge. What do you want to do - fish? dive?"

"Both. What's this thing weigh?" Djinni knew what he needed.

"The tandem model is ninety-five pounds."

"You got anything lighter - inflatable?"

"Yup. Over here." Djinni and Hakeem followed Rick to the inflatable display.

"The tandem inflatable weighs forty-five pounds and can carry two men plus four hundred pounds of gear. Some of the mountaineering clubs use these for excursions into Alaska and long range trips on the Columbia River."

"How about a motor and transom for this model?"

"Yes, sir. No problem. Same motor - two horse. She'll do sixty miles at five knots."

"Give us a moment to discuss it. Come with me, Hakeem. Let's go sit in the truck and review our options."

Hakeem didn't know what Djinni was thinking. All this kayak information didn't seem to fit the overall plan.

"Why are we looking at kayaks? I thought we were going to use your power boat?"

"Change of plans. I sold it. Too noisy. Listen, Hakeem. We have two important missions to carry out simultaneously. Ziad and Khalid will attack the induction pipeline. You and I will attack the nuclear waste storage site - blow a hole in the canisters - make giant dirty bombs. Both attacks will please Allah."

Djinni took an extra moment to consider the best possible means to transport the men and equipment. Stealth and speed were the highest priorities.

"Motorized inflatables," Djinni yelled.

"What about Osaman?"

"He has another mission. Besides, we don't need him."

****

Late the following afternoon, Djinni called Osaman.

"This is Djnni. Meet me at the coffee shop in one hour. Don't be late."

Osaman was standing outside when Djinni drove up. The sun had just sunk below the horizon, painting an orange glow across the western sky.

"Where's Hakeem?"

"He's in his apartment. We don't need him tonight. I want to show you our insertion point. Jump in. I'll take you there."

"Where is this place?"

"You'll see. Not far. Up the coast. A quiet lagoon with ocean access. Sixteen miles south of our target."

The sun had disappeared below the horizon when Djinni pulled into the narrow road leading to the Batiquitos Lagoon and Nature Preserve. The tide was out, exposing the naked bottom and the slimy critters that called its muddy bottom home.

"Come on. Let me show you where we're going to launch our operation. I want your opinion."

Osaman followed Djinni down to the tidal flats, looking out over the hilly sandstone landscape and shoreline of the lagoon for signs of activity. There were none.

"Hey, this place is pretty deserted. But it's a long way to Ortega. It's not sixteen miles to the target - it's more like thirty."

Osaman turned to look back toward the Interstate. As he watched the rush hour traffic bump and grind its way home, Djinni retrieved his silenced automatic pistol - took aim - and fired a single bullet into the back of Osaman's head.

Djinni looked up to the darkening sky while returning his weapon to his pocket. "Allahu Akbar," he said as he proceeded to pull Osaman's body across the muddy bottom.

Soon the incoming tide would wash his body to the far end of the lagoon where it would remain until the smell of his decaying flesh was reported by a local nature lover.

"That's payback for losing Ramin. And we don't need more than two boats for this mission."

MAGNETS

Greg stood at the head of the long conference table. Allan Rusk, Warrant Officer Cliff Brady (EOD), Gordon Paris, CEO of Blue-star Security, and Richard Winslow, the Ortega security chief, sat to his right. April Mason, Lieutenant Scott Lewis, OIC of the SEAL vet-tech platoon, and Navy Chiefs Pace and Wagner sat to his left.

"Good morning. You've all been briefed on the situation we're facing at the Ortega nuclear power plant. We strongly believe a small group of jihadists plan to attack the cooling system and create a Fukushima type meltdown." Greg paused to let the enormity of this terrorist threat invade every nerve and receptor in the audience.

"While we believe our threat assessment is accurate, there is always the possibility we have made an error in some facet or another. Additionally, we don't have all the information needed to mount effective countermeasures. So for the moment, we're still gathering data while implementing a DEFCON FOUR condition. That means our assets are ready to engage the enemy on four hours' notice. Gordon, what are your patrol recommendations?"

"Richard and I discussed this at length. We believe the best we can do is monitor the restricted area with hourly helicopter flights. The flight crew will make video runs over the restricted area using FLIR and night vision equipment. The video feed will be transmitted to the Ortega security station and archived for future review. We estimate the flight time to be approximately twenty minutes. Additionally, we plan to double the head count in the security control room."

"Great. Lieutenant, what is your current game plan?"

"We'll put two DSBs on standby. Each boat will have a four-man SEAL Combat Craft crew, two SEAL vet-techs, a couple of dolphins, plus a *Songbook* operator."

"Allan, where will X-ray and Brady be in the event of an EOD requirement?"

"They'll remain on DEFCON FOUR as will our helicopter flight crew. Brady has a full set of the latest EOD gear - arthroscopic type tools designed specifically for bomb disposal applications - endoscopes, a pulsed diode laser cutter-driller, quick-set insulating epoxy injector, and more. They can be over Ortega in thirty minutes."

"Excellent. April, what have you got?"

"Chiefs Pace and Wagner will be on standby. They will join us on the helicopter if and when we are called. They each have DULAN underwater communication units. Adam and X-ray can deploy by helicopter. Dolphins Uno and Luke will be assigned to the DSB."

"Excellent. Any questions?"

"I assume these terrorists are planning to swim up the induction pipeline. Is that correct?" asked Brady.

"I don't know how else they could get inside."

"Yeah, but you know there's almost three billion gallons of seawater sucked into that pipe every day. I'm no math wizard, but that water is flowing pretty fast. It's not a problem getting in - but getting out is a totally different kettle of fish. Divers cannot swim against the incoming current. Maybe they know that and don't plan to escape, or have high-speed propulsion systems. Furthermore, once inside the pipe there's no stopping the current from pulling them directly into the rotating biological intervention screen - where they'd be crushed to death."

"We know they purchased some underwater propulsion units capable of three knots. I'd say that's evidence they intend to escape. But you're right about the current. I have no idea how they could stay in a fixed location for more than a few seconds - unless of course, they had some means to attach themselves to the inside of the pipeline."

"Magnets, neodymium magnets!" Brady cried out. "The inside of the pipe is steel."

Everyone looked around the room for consensus. "That's it!" exclaimed Allan, pumping his arm. "Brady, see if you can locate a magnet capable of stabilizing a diver inside a steel pipe against a current."

"Already did. Bought a half dozen of them yesterday. They have an eyelet to accept a carabiner."

"Sounds like we're good to go. Stay alert, people. All we can do now is watch over the area and be ready to respond immediately."

SANTA MARGARITA CREEK

The pounding on his door woke Hakeem from an afternoon nap. Damn, it must be Djinni. "I'm coming," he shouted, rubbing his eyes. "Stop beating on my door."

Upon opening the door, Djinni barked, "Quick, come with me. Ziad and Khalid are already downstairs. We've got work to do."

"What's the rush? It's Saturday."

"Bring your jacket. That's all you'll need today."

Hakeem grabbed his jacket and followed Djinni to the parking lot.

"Sit in the back."

"But Ziad and Khalid are there. Why can't I sit up front with you?"

"Get ... in... the... back! Why do I always have to repeat myself?" Djinni raised his head upward. "Please, Allah. Oh, never mind."

"Okay, Djinni. Okay, I get it. Why are you so damn miserable?" Hakeem was annoyed with Djinni's constant criticism. "And where is Osaman?"

Djinni gave Hakeem a hard glare. "As the Americans say, 'he got cold feet.' He went back to Grozny to be with what's left of his family after the Chechen wars. Anyway, we don't need him."

Not wishing to engage Djinni in a debate over Osaman, Hakeem squeezed into the back seat as Djinni had ordered. .

"Where are we going?" asked Ziad.

Djinni put the truck in gear and headed for the exit.

"Launch site. I'll explain more when we get there. But first I've got to stop at Manny's Fish Market."

"What for?" asked Ziad.

"Lobsters. Two big lobsters."

The men looked at each other and shrugged their shoulders, wondering if Djinni was having some sort of breakdown. Minutes later, he pulled up to Manny's Fish Market.

"I'll be right back." Djinni sounded more like his normal grump.

"Maybe he just has a craving for lobsters," said Ziad condescendingly.

Djinni quickly returned, opened the rear door and tossed a white paper package to Ziad.

"You're in charge of the lobsters." Ziad thought it wise to refrain from asking more lobster questions.

Djinni took the Interstate toward Camp Pendleton exiting onto Vandergrift Street and following the two-lane road for three miles past the back gate before turning left on a narrow dirt road. The whitewashed signpost read Stuart Mesa Trail. No one dared ask Djinni where he was taking them. However, they could easily see headlights from the eight lanes of Interstate traffic in the distance.

Djinni continued down the narrowing trail until he was directly under the Interstate overpass. He turned off the road into a patch of black sage, willows, and scrub oaks. After several twists and turns, he stopped at the edge of a lagoon.

"Everyone out."

"Where are we?" asked Ziad.

"Santa Margarita Creek. It leads to the ocean. We'll launch our inflatable kayaks from here, and then motor out to sea and up the coast. We're only an hour from the plant. We're going to rehearse our insertion and test the reaction time of the Ortega security."

"Oh, I get it. This is a reconnaissance mission."

"Yeah, it's critical too. So follow my instructions - and no more stupid questions - please." Djinni was clearly agitated. "All right, I know. You're wondering about the lobsters, right?"

Still baffled, the men nodded simultaneously.

"Well, you're going to pretend you captured them. If the security helicopter shows up, we'll tell them we're diving for lobsters and show them our catch. We'll repeat this exercise tomorrow for the next few nights. As long as we stay outside the restricted area, they won't force us to leave. We'll also run a test inside the restricted area and note how long it takes for them to discover our presence. I'm sure they'll order us to leave. We'll show them our lobsters and leave."

COUNTDOWN

Tuesday, 7:20 PM (1920 hours)

There was that pounding on the door again. Hakeem had just finished his evening meal.

"What does he want now?" Hakeem mumbled. "I'm coming. I'm coming."

Djinni knocked again - three loud poundings.

Hakeem unlocked the door. Djinni rushed inside, a sense of urgency washed across his face.

"We've got to go now! Can't wait for the new moon. We've got to go tonight!"

"Why the change of plans?"

"Sea fog. The forecast is for a dense fog tonight until midday tomorrow. There will be no light - not even a twinkle of starlight. The security helicopter can't fly in this shit. We've got to go tonight. Get dressed and grab the drone and fresh batteries. I have the shape charges in the truck."

Djinni rushed down the passageway to rouse Ziad and Khalid. They had a separate apartment from Hakeem; cultural differences prevented them from residing in the same unit.

"Open up. It's me. Open the door!"

Ziad rose from the couch where he'd been dozing.

"Who's there?" he yelled.

"It's me, open the fucking door."

Ziad unlocked the door. Djinni gave him an evil stare as he rushed into the apartment.

"What do you want?" asked Ziad sheepishly.

"Get dressed and grab all your gear. You and Khalid are going diving tonight. The weather is predicted to be foggy - sea fog - the kind that drifts just above the water. There is no visibility - perfect for your mission. Where's Khalid?"

"In the bedroom. He's been drinking - partying like a teenage infidel on spring break."

"Well, go wake him up and tell him to pack his gear. Make sure you install a fresh oxygen bottle and change the carbon dioxide absorbent!"

"That will only take a minute or two. Where are we going?"

"Santa Margarita Creek. We're attacking tonight."

Djinni strutted into the bedroom to wake up Khalid while Ziad exchanged his half empty oxygen bottle for a full one and replaced the carbon dioxide absorbent.

Khalid shuffled from the bedroom rubbing his eyes. Djinni slapped him - first on his butt, then on the back of his head. "Come on. Get your shit together. You're going to die for Allah tonight."

"Hey, Khalid. Give me your re-breather. I'll put in a fresh oxygen bottle and replace the absorbent for you while you dress and get your gear packed. We probably won't be back." Believing tonight might be his last before ascending to heaven and receiving his seven blessings, Ziad had the jabbering jitters.

****

Djinni turned off the Interstate onto Vandergrift Street toward Santa Margarita Creek. Unlike most nights, the air was thick and humid. An endless parade of flying insects buzzed in and out of the headlight beams as they made their way to the launch site. A light haze blanketed across the sky. He turned onto Stuart Mesa Trail and continued down the dirt track until he was directly under the Interstate overpass. He turned off the path, winding his way through patches of vegetation, and stopped at the edge of the lagoon.

"Okay, here we are. It's nine fifteen." Djinni looked up into the haze. "Perfect," he snickered. "Let's inflate our kayaks and rig the motors. We've got no time to spare. I want to be at the dive site by midnight. But before we depart, I need to give each of you a *shahid* grenade."

"A *shahid* grenade! Why? I thought we were going to die martyrs completing our mission. Isn't that what Allah wants?"

"That is certainly the preferred route to martyrdom. But Allah grants every jihadist his blessings if he dies before, during, or immediately after his mission. Allah does not bestow his blessings on cowards. It is not suicide. You are *shahid* - an attacker - a holy warrior destined for martyrdom. Your mission is of primary importance and your death is mandatory. Otherwise, your spirit will forever remain in *al-Barzakh*, a place between heaven and hell. You cannot be captured. The infidels will send you to Guantanamo prison where you'll spend the rest of your days being tortured, with no possibility of receiving your seven blessings."

Without saying a word, Hakeem held out his hand. Djinni took a silvery metal tube from his backpack and handed it to Hakeem.

"Here, watch me. I will show you how easy it is. See, it's about the same size as a cigarette lighter with a flip-top cap." Djinni flipped the device open. "There are three numbered dials. Turn them to the number 666. That translates into the ancient Arabic word *Bismillah* or *in the name of Allah*."

"Then what?" Ziad asked nervously.

"Hold it against your head or chest and press the red button."

"That's all there is to it?" Hakeem's eyes widened.

"You won't feel a thing. I promise."

Hakeem held it in his hand, running his fingers over the smooth metal surface - feeling its deadly power - letting the thought of martyring himself settle into his psyche.

Djinni removed three more *shahid* grenades, ceremoniously placing one in the outstretched palms of Ziad and Khalid. As a final gesture of solidarity, Djinni kissed the last *shahid* grenade and placed it in his pocket.

"Okay. Let's get busy. We have a long and fateful night ahead of us."

Hakeem pulled his inflatable kayak from the truck, connected the air pump to the cigarette lighter outlet and began to inflate his kayak. He then prepared the motor mount and battery.

"Hurry up, Hakeem. What's taking you so long?" shouted Ziad ramping up his contempt for Hakeem.

"I've got to inflate my kayak. It's the pump, stupid. It's slow. If you're in such a hurry why don't you blow it up with your big mouth?"

"Fuck you!" Ziad shouted. Eager to regain his arrogant authority, he went face to face with Hakeem.

"Hey, you two. Stop screwing around." Djinni stepped between the quarrelsome jihadists. "We're on a mission. You can defend your honor in heaven. Allah can be the referee. Maybe the winner will get an extra virgin."

Ziad and Khalid put on their wetsuits, gloves, and dive booties and loaded their diving equipment and four-piece shaped charge into their kayak.

Djinni and Hakeem secured the propulsion units, drone, and four drone bombs in their kayak.

"Everyone ready? Follow me." Djinni and Hakeem launched their kayak followed by Ziad and Khalid. A layer of mist hung over the lagoon, foretelling a thick blanket of sea fog would soon descend upon them.

****

Tuesday, 11:20 PM (2320 hours)
After departing Santa Margarita Creek, it would not be long until they crossed the sand bar from the lagoon to the open ocean. They would then motor north until, according to their GPS coordinates, they had reached the dive site.

As they cruised up the coast, Hakeem was brought back in time to when he and his brother Ramin went off to college. The Sheik and his son Abdul had paved the way - helping them obtain the appropriate counterfeit documentation needed to attend Berkeley and paying for an apartment near the campus.

As a teen, Hakeem yearned to be a nuclear physicist. But somewhere along the way, he began to lose interest. After his father was killed by the infidels, the rage inside him took over. What he now wanted most was revenge. So in many ways, it was a blessing from Allah when Djinni came into his life providing the means and motivation to complete his jihad.

****

Wednesday, 12:15 AM (0015 hours)
By the time they reached the dive site, the invading fog had reduced visibility to a few feet. The sea was breathless. Rolling swells passed silently under the keels of the inflatable kayaks while a thousand yards to the east, insignificant waves breached the shores of Ortega beach.

On a clear night, the lights of the power plant outlined the reactor buildings - two grandiose hemispherical containment structures with barrel-size nipples reaching upwards like a pair of magnificent boobs - each nipple tipped with a twinkling red navigation light.

"Get dressed in your dive gear. Allah is waiting. Set the shaped charge detonator for twenty-four hours."

Ziad and Khalid slipped on their re-breathers and entered the water. While they treaded water, Djinni attached two of the four sections of the shaped charge to each propulsion unit and then carefully lowered them to the waiting divers.

"You're outside the restricted zone. The entrance to the induction pipe is about twenty-eight hundred feet from here. Set your compass heading for three hundred and twenty degrees. You'll see the dark spherical shadow of the entrance to the pipe in about ten minutes. Oh, and one more thing. Stay away from the La Jolla Trench. It will be to your left."

There was a moment of uneasy silence as Ziad and Khalid bit down forcefully on their mouthpieces, turned on their flashlights and set their compass course. Gripping their underwater scooters, they quietly submerged. As he watched the water collapse over their bubble-free descent, Hakeem had a sudden rush of anxiety - a sobering flash of uncertainty. How would he die? Would he receive Allah's seven blessings?

"How long do we have to wait?" he asked.

Djinni replied, "Not long."

****

Khalid was the first to see the dark opening of the induction pipeline. He tugged on Ziad's shoulder and pointed toward the entrance. Ziad nodded and they shortly began to feel the current sucking them into the pipe. Ziad pushed the anchor spike of the running line into the sand and began to spool off line indicating their distance from the entrance.

Their journey down the pipe was dark, almost spiritual. As they approached the target, each diver readied his neodymium magnet. When they reached their designated location, both divers slapped their magnet to the pipe. Fixed to their magnets by a short length of rope, they were able to remain in position. They let their propulsion units swing freely at the end of a tether and proceeded to assemble the shaped charge.

Ziad attached his two-piece sub-assembly to the uppermost interior wall of the pipe and turned to assist Khalid. Khalid positioned his sub-assembly and the detonator against the pipe while Ziad attached a magnet at each corner, forming a perfectly square shaped charge.

When finished, they looked back for a final inspection of their deadly undertaking. Ziad placed his flashlight under his chin illuminating a bittersweet expression. He gave Khalid a consolatory grin and turned the dial on the detonator timer for twenty-four hours. Both divers checked their watches. It was twenty minutes past one in the morning.

****

Wednesday, 1:21 AM (0121 hours)

The Chechen divers retrieved their propulsion units and disconnected themselves from the magnets. Turning toward the pipe entrance, they applied full power. The force of the incoming water pressed against their faces. Ziad looked at his watch and checked his battery level.

Shortly after commencing their return, Khalid's propulsion unit began to slow. His battery level had entered the red zone. He began to kick with all his strength knowing that by doing so, he would overwork his carbon dioxide absorbent. The buildup of carbon dioxide could be deadly. Nevertheless, he was determined to get out of the pipe and continued to kick as forcefully as his legs and lungs would permit.

Ziad exited the pipe and looked back to see if Khalid was nearby. Sensing his dive partner was in trouble, he grabbed the running line and began to pull - hoping Khalid would likewise take a grip on the line and pull himself to the exit.

Khalid's propulsion unit suddenly stopped well short of the exit. Distraught at the thought of perishing inside the induction pipe, he repeatedly pulled the throttle trigger.

He instantly felt his body drift back toward the pump room. He struggled with all his might to swim in the opposite direction - arms pulling, legs kicking - but the force of the incoming water was overwhelming. Frantically, he tried to claw his way out of the steel coffin, but it was futile. His carbon dioxide absorbent had been depleted. His heart raced - his senses numbed. Suffering from extreme vertigo, he began to turn in circles. Unable to get his bearings, he drifted deeper into the pipe.

Somewhere in the darkness of the induction pipe, Khalid passed out. Without muscle control and a forceful grip, he lost his mouthpiece. His breathing bag quickly filled with seawater. He sank to the bottom of the pipe where the current steadily tumbled his lifeless body toward the Ortega pump room.

Ziad surfaced and filled his breathing bag to the limit. Nothing could be seen but dense white fog. He thought about swimming, but he had no clue as to which way to go. Besides, he was too exhausted to fight the outgoing tide and prevailing current.

Alone and lost in the fog, he drifted with the tide and current.

****

Wednesday, 3:30 AM (0330 hours)

"Where are those divers?"

Djinni had not planned on losing them. It was too foggy to see more than a few feet in any direction. He and Hakeem spent a couple of hours scanning the surface of the ocean with their flashlights.

"Maybe they got caught or ran out of gas?" Hakeem began to shake with the thought of dying inside such a dark and dreadful place. "We don't know if they attached their shaped charge or when the device is expected to detonate. What are we going to do now?"

Djinni shook his head while steering his kayak in circles, calling out, "Ziad. Khalid. Can you hear me?" A lone seagull glided above them, squawking loudly. Other than the splashing of water against the rubberized fabric of the inflatables, the sea was silent.

"What are we going to do? How am I supposed to fly a drone

in this fog? I can't see fuck all!" Hakeem cried out in frustration.

Djinni leaned back against the port side of his kayak to contemplate the situation. After a few minutes, he regained his resolve.

"I'm going to search for the divers. You stay put."

"But what if you get lost in this fog. What am I to do?"

"I've got a GPS. I'll come back to you. We can't leave now. We have to wait until the sun burns the fog off - then launch the drone. Yeah, that's what we'll do. Wait until the fog lifts - then kill them all. I'm sure Ziad and Khalid were successful. Their charge should detonate early tomorrow morning. Let us pray to Allah for victory and honor."

****

Wednesday, 5:30 AM (0530 hours)

Greg rolled over and looked at his watch. He couldn't go back to sleep; there were far too many troublesome images tracing figure eights in his head. He pulled on his trousers and hobbled to the kitchen to make a pot of coffee. Most of the base personnel were still asleep. But not BUD/S - SEAL trainees.

The SEAL training area was lit up like a new car lot. "Must be Hell Week," Greg surmised. "I wonder if it has changed much since my time thirty years ago. Damn, those were great times - brutal and painful to the core, but worth every minute."

After pouring himself a cup of coffee, he settled into the couch and drifted off to the first time he and April made love. It was a magical moment. They were in the middle of a conversation when she boldly took him by the hand and waltzed him into his bedroom. The memory of their first encounter brought a tiny tear of joy to each eye. "God, I love that woman."

His romantic musings trailed off to a more sinister subject - the real threat of a nuclear meltdown at the Ortega nuclear power plant.

He knew the gory details and loss of life in the aftermath

of the Fukushima disaster. Would Southern California be next? That thought brought a lump to his throat and a gasp of trepidation.

The Fukushima calamity was eleven years ago and those responsible had made no progress in reducing the radiation leaks. In fact, it was much worse.

The uninhabitable area grew from eighty to one hundred thousand square miles - displacing tens of millions of people. Deaths from thyroid and lung cancer had quadrupled. Infant mortality increased five hundred percent. Unspeakable newborn deformities ripped the soul from heartbroken mothers and fathers.

The Fukushima on site personnel had done everything possible to regain control of the situation. They desperately tried to start the backup generators, but they were made useless by the invasion of seawater. They closed off every manual valve and sealed every compartment to contain radioactive contamination. In spite of their efforts to mitigate the problem, every measure was futile. Without electrical power, the cooling pumps - the lifeline for the entire plant - shut down. Without water, the reactor cores began to overheat at a rate of one degree Fahrenheit *per second.*

****

The meltdown cycle commenced ten hours after the tsunami knocked out the power to the cooling water pumps. The realization of an impending meltdown was not widely known - only the shift supervisors and a few of the control engineers understood the worst possible catastrophe was imminent. There was nothing they could do but watch the core temperature rising inside the reactor chambers - and pray.

Some emergency procedures went into effect before the electrical power was lost. Control rods were automatically inserted to slow down the fission reaction - but without cooling water the zirconium-clad control rods gradually oxidized and disintegrated.

By the time the reactor temperature had climbed to 1,500 degrees Fahrenheit, the zirconium cladding began to bulge and crack. By contrast, volcanic lava turned from a solid to a liquid at 1,300 degrees.

At one degree increase in temperature every second, it took only seventeen minutes for the temperature to increase from 1,500 to 2,500 degrees - more than doubling the rate of zircaloy oxidation and creating huge volumes of hydrogen - enough to make a sizeable bomb.

Unable to contain the ever rising temperature and hydrogen buildup, the containment vessels exploded, sending molten radioactive debris and gas into the atmosphere. The wind spread the lethal contamination over the surrounding area. However, the main event - the demon of all demons - the ultimate - was yet to come.

It took less than an hour for the temperature of the molten material to reach 6,000 degrees - *alpha mode failure* they called it. At that point, the prodigious glob of radioactive material penetrated the base of the containment vessel and began to burn its way into the earth's crust. It would eventually reach the mantle but for the ground water flowing under the Fukushima power plant. This cold underground river re-solidified the radioactive glob, preventing it from flowing further into the earth's crust.

Greg envisioned a similar apocalypse in Southern California. Ground water would cool the demonic blob into a semi-solid mass while millions of gallons of virulent radioactive water flowed into the sea each day. The radiation levels in the ocean would continue rising, poisoning the fish, animals, and all the marine creatures that depended on it for food and reproduction. As for Ortega, a meltdown on the order of Fukushima would eventually kill tens of thousands of people and turn Southern California into a wasteland. The never-ending outflow of radiation would continue until humans found a way to contain it - best estimates being - *nobody really knows.*

****

Dressed in her flimsiest nightie, April sauntered into the kitchen pulling her fingers through her long blond hair. She let out an elongated yawn and looked out the window.

"You're up early. What's bugging you?"

"How about a cup of coffee?" asked Greg. He would have preferred to take her back to bed, but the wrath of Fukushima festered in his thoughts.

"Sit tight. I'll get it."

"Come, sit down with me on the couch. We need to have a chat."

Taking a sip of her hot coffee, April sat next to her husband, tucking her naked legs under her derriere.

"This situation is disturbing. The threat of a terrorist assault on Ortega is quite plausible. There have been numerous warnings. And we all know how complacent the security services tend to be - especially after midnight. It could get out of control - very dangerous for you if…."

"Hey, if you're trying to suggest I shouldn't be with you in this operation… well, forget about it. This is what I do. This is what our magnanimous dolphin partners do - help rid the world of criminals and terrorists. Don't forget, I'm an Annapolis graduate and former commander in the Navy. Am I scared? Certainly. But I'm also responsible and accountable." April's jaw tightened; her eyes narrowed. There was no doubt she meant every word.

"I just wanted you to know how deadly things could get. If the worst happens, it will be over in a matter of minutes - there would be no escaping the terror of it all. The dolphins will likely avoid the heaviest dose of radiation by being in the water and swimming away from the area. We don't have that option.

115

We're talking minutes, April - not hours or days. If the terrorists somehow manage to cause a nuclear accident - even a relatively minor one - the area could very well become unlivable." Greg reached out and touched her arm. "I could never forgive myself if you were injured or killed. I love you too much."

April put down her coffee and snuggled up to Greg. "I love you too. You are my world. But I'm not afraid to die. We all go there - wherever that is. I'm terrified of losing you." She softly kissed Greg on the lips. As Greg prepared to speak, she placed her right index finger over his mouth and whispered, "Shh."

The ring tone of Greg's cell phone broke the silence.

"Hello."

"Greg?"

"Yes. Who is this?"

"Richard Winslow, Ortega head of security. Sorry if I woke you."

"As a matter of fact, I've been up for some time. What's going on?" A chill raced up his spine. "Do we have a breach?" He held his breath.

"I don't know, but you need to see what we captured on our one AM Monday morning flyover. I'll email the video to you."

"Monday morning! It's Wednesday morning! Are your people asleep at the wheel? This should have been brought to our attention immediately. Goddamn it. Yes, please. Send it immediately. I'll call you back after viewing it and consider our next move. Thanks, Richard, but you need to speak with your chopper pilots and security staff." As Greg hung up the phone he gave April an ominous grimace.

"April, honey. That was Richard Winslow. He's got some video they took two nights ago on a helicopter flyover. He's emailing it to me now. Let's watch it together."

"Okay. What about Allan?"

"Yeah, he needs to see it too. Let's see what we're dealing with, then I'll call him."

After downloading the video file, Greg pressed the play button. Two inflatable kayaks appeared floating on the ocean. There was one man in each boat and two free divers hanging onto the side. Each diver wore a wetsuit, mask, fins, and snorkel. There was no scuba gear.

The force of the rotor created an avalanche of sea spray across the faces of the men in the kayaks and they held up an arm to shield their eyes from the barrage of salt water and intensity of the helicopter searchlight.

"Turn up the volume a bit," asked April.

Greg and April could hear the roar of the helicopter in the background and the voice coming over the bullhorn. "You have entered a restricted zone," the security officer shouted. "Please depart immediately. This area is off limits to all private watercraft."

"We're just diving for lobsters," shouted one of the men, covering his face from the stinging maelstrom.

Suddenly Greg stopped the video. "That's our guy - the man with the eye patch. The Ortega security helicopter got him on video several weeks ago. He was in a Grady- White. The FBI tried to ID the guy but have not had any luck."

Greg replayed the scene.

"We're just diving for lobsters." The man covered his face then quickly looked down, turning his face away from the camera.

"There. Just for a fraction of a second. You can see it - there's a black patch over his left eye."

"Play it back once more," asked April. "Stop. Back up a few frames. There he is. Our one-eyed terrorist."

Greg continued to play the rest of the video. An unidentified man in the second inflatable shouted, "We're diving for lobsters." He picked up a large lobster and held it high above his head. "We've got a license."

"You must leave this area immediately or we will call the

Coast Guard. You will be cited for trespassing in a restricted area. Please leave this area at once."

The man showing off the lobsters yelled out, "Okay, we're leaving."

The divers clambered into the kayaks and headed south toward Camp Pendleton. The helicopter followed them for a few minutes, then broke contact.

"They were using electrical outboard motors. Now, why would they do that?" April asked.

"Stealth. Electrical outboard motors are very quiet - the acoustical signature is virtually impossible for our sonar to detect. Professional bass fishermen use them to sneak up on their trophy lunkers."

"That's what our dolphins do better than humans - hear underwater noises better than any man-made sonar." April took another sip of her coffee while Greg called Allan.

"Allan, sorry to wake you but you need to come to the guest house immediately. We've got a disturbing security video from Ortega."

"I'm on my way."

Wrapping his arms around April's waist he pulled her close and buried his head against her soft neck. He kissed her several times from her shoulder to her earlobe then pulled away with a tenderhearted expression.

"There's nothing I can or would do to stop you from doing your job. Promise me you'll be careful. Promise me if the worst happens you'll leave the contaminated area as quickly as possible."

"I promise - as long as you promise the same for me. We are not combatants. We're not first responders to a nuclear disaster. We're not trained or prepared to deal with a meltdown. We'll round up our dolphins and leave the area. Agreed?"

"Agreed."

There was a knock on the door.

"Come on in, Allan!" shouted Greg.

"Hey, good morning. What's going on?"

"We're just about ready to watch this video for the umpteenth time. Sit down and give us your thoughts."

Greg replayed the video, looking for more clues.

"You have entered a restricted zone. Please depart immediately. This area is off limits to all private watercraft."

"We're diving for lobsters. We've got a license."

Greg froze the image of the one-eyed man looking up at the helicopter.

"Allan, look closely. That's our mystery man - the guy with the eye patch - covering his face. He's paid numerous visits to the restricted zone in a Grady-White. Always claimed to be fishing and departed. These kayaks are new. So is the diving. I'll take some screen shots and get them out to the team."

Greg restarted the video.

"We're diving for lobsters. We've got a license."

"You must leave this area immediately or we will call the Coast Guard. You will be cited for trespassing in a restricted area. Please leave this area at once."

"Okay, we're leaving."

Greg stopped the video.

"Have you spoken to the helicopter pilot?" asked Allan.

"Not yet," replied Greg.

"We need to ask him some questions."

"Go back to the lobsters. Something is not kosher." Allan had a premonition.

Greg replayed the video.

"I don't believe it." Allan shook his head.

"Don't believe what?" April suddenly became apprehensive.

"Those lobsters have claws. Those are cold water lobsters from Maine. The California spiny lobsters are a different species. They're considered warm water lobsters - *and they don't have claws*."

"Goddamn it. You're right, Allan. I missed that. Anything else?"

"Yeah. I want to speak with the helicopter pilot."

Greg dialed plant security. Richard answered the phone.

"Richard, Greg Mason here. I've got Allan Rusk and April with me. We need to speak with your helicopter pilot who took the video. Please ask him to call me immediately."

"That will be Billy Reynolds. I'll call him right away. Was the video helpful?"

"Oh, yeah. It shows the same guy with the black eye patch that has been nosing around Ortega for weeks."

"Why did he stop using the Grady-White? It's certainly bigger and faster than a couple of battery-powered kayaks."

"There's really only one reason - stealth. Please ask the pilot to call me ASAP."

****

Greg snatched up his phone on the first ringtone. "Hello. This is Greg."

"This is Billy Reynolds. I'm the chief pilot for Bluestar. Richard asked me to call you about these men in kayaks."

"Thanks for calling. Hold tight while I put you on the speaker - there's a couple of people here that want to hear our call. Have you previously seen these divers and inflatable kayaks inside or outside the restricted zone?"

"They showed up three consecutive nights - four men - two free divers dressed in wetsuits - one man in each kayak. The first and second time they remained outside the restricted zone and we warned them. The third night - Monday morning, just after midnight, we video recorded them inside the restricted zone. Both divers were in the water. They said they were free diving for lobsters and showed them to us. We told them to leave and they did."

"Billy, what was your exact location when you spotted the

kayaks - your precise location?"

"About twelve hundred yards off the beach. I can probably provide the GPS data if you wish."

"Were you over the La Jolla Trench?"

"Absolutely. The trench runs parallel to the beach from Dana Point to La Jolla. It's over a thousand feet deep - too deep for lobster diving."

"When is the next new moon - the darkest night of the month?"

"Give me a moment to check my lunar calendar... tomorrow night."

"Thanks, Billy. You've been a great help." Greg hung up his phone.

"We must mobilize immediately - put our dolphin sentries in the water. We'll need Brady and X-ray too. I'll call Ortega security and let them know what's going on. April, you take charge of mobilizing the dolphins. I will meet you at the heliport."

"Do you want Brady and X-ray to go with us?" asked Allan.

"Not now. Just get them ready. We need to figure out how to get them to Ortega and how and where to put them when they arrive. And check on the weather. It's clear here, but who knows what it's like up the coast."

April checked the NOAA website for the latest weather forecast along the Ortega coastline. It was disturbing news.

"Ortega is socked in - a huge blanket of sea fog. We're not going anywhere this morning. Sea fog extends from Long Beach to Oceanside - thick as cream cheese. They say it should lift by early afternoon. We might be able to truck a couple of dolphins to patrol the area."

"Get dressed. We've got to move quickly. This could get very dicey."

The adrenaline rushed into Greg's brain, kicking his thinking into overdrive. It had been over a year since the last emergency involving his talking dolphins and Navy SEALs. The very thought of engaging terrorists in Southern California spiked his temperament, bringing back the days when he too was an active duty SEAL operator.

Nothing about the SEALs had changed since those days thirty years ago. BUD/S was still the toughest military training in the world. Its graduates were dedicated, resilient and highly effective warriors capable of engaging America's enemies at sea, in the air, or on land. Their brotherhood inspired them to accomplish deadly missions that no others could achieve. Their SEAL Ethos sealed their commitment to their country and to their teammates.

****

SEAL ETHOS

In times of war or uncertainty, there is a special breed of warrior ready to answer our Nation's call - a common man with uncommon desire to succeed. Forged by adversity, he stands alongside America's finest special operations forces to serve his country, the American people, and protect their way of life. I am that man.

My Trident is a symbol of honor and heritage. Bestowed upon me by the heroes that have gone before, it embodies the trust of those I have sworn to protect. By wearing the Trident I accept the responsibility of my chosen profession and way of life. It is a privilege that I must earn every day. My loyalty to Country and Team is beyond reproach. I humbly serve as a guardian to my fellow Americans always ready to defend those who are unable to defend themselves. I do not advertise the nature of my work, nor seek recognition for my actions. I voluntarily accept the inherent hazards of my profession, placing the welfare and security of others before my own. I serve with honor on and off the battlefield. The ability to control my emotions and my actions, regardless of circumstance, sets me apart from other men. Uncompromising integrity is my standard. My character and honor are steadfast. My word is my bond.

We expect to lead and be led. In the absence of orders, I will take charge, lead my teammates and accomplish the mission. I lead by example in all situations. I will never quit. I persevere and thrive on adversity. My Nation expects me to be physically harder and mentally stronger than my enemies. If knocked down, I will get back up, every time. I will draw on every remaining ounce of strength to protect my teammates and to accomplish our mission. I am never out of the fight.

We demand discipline. We expect innovation. The lives of my teammates and the success of our mission depend on me – my technical skill, tactical proficiency, and attention to detail. My training is never complete. We train for war and fight to win. I stand ready to bring the full spectrum of combat power to bear in order to achieve my mission and the goals established by my country. The execution of my duties will be swift and violent when required yet guided by the very principles that I serve to defend. Brave men have fought and died building the proud tradition and feared reputation that I am bound to uphold. In the worst of conditions, the legacy of my teammates steadies my resolve and silently guides my every deed. I will not fail.

LOST IN A SEA OF FOG

Wednesday, 5:35 AM (0535 hours)

Ziad's wetsuit had done its job. But after being submerged in the ocean for six hours, hypothermia had ultimately worked its way into his core. His body and lower jaw shivered uncontrollably. With no visible landmarks as reference points, Ziad could not get his bearings. Hoping to determine the direction of the beach, he listened for the sound of waves breaking on the shoreline. The only sound was from a cresting swell splashing against his face.

The occasional sea bird flying inches above the water gave him no comfort. Small cleaner fish had gathered around him, dashing about his arms and legs seeking specks of plankton stuck to his diving equipment. To them, Ziad was a piece of flotsam - a sanctuary from predators and a source of food.

His teeth began to chatter. Fighting off the debilitating effects of the cold water, he bit down hard on his lower lip; blood oozed into his mouth and the sea. For a brief moment, the chattering ceased - seconds later it returned.

"Allahu Akbar!" he shouted. "Take me to your house of pleasure. I am a faithful jihadist. I have done my duty. Praise Allah. King of all Kings, Lord of all Lords. Take me to paradise."

Suddenly, they arrived and began to circle. First one - then two and three.

Ziad spun around, trying to keep his eyes on the leader - the one nearest his face - the one with an erect dorsal fin protruding from the surface and rubbing his slender body against his torso. The pack circled menacingly, sensing a meal. He tried to swim away, but he was exhausted - chilled to the bone - devoid of fighting spirit.

A rush of adrenaline-laced terror shot up his spine and into his belly. Suddenly he was nauseated and immediately vomited. He did his best to calm his nerves, but there was no stopping the school of sharks. Their predatory instincts took control of their small brains and drove them toward their prey. There was a meal to be had and they were not to be denied. He looked up and cried out, "Allahu Akbar. I am ready."

Suddenly, almost by magic, the pack of blue sharks disappeared into the depths.

Puzzled, Ziad lowered his face into the water. The sharks were nowhere in sight. Even the cleaner fish had abandoned him. Except for his pounding heartbeat, it was eerily silent.

Out of the corner of his right eye, he saw the shadow of the colossal beast closing in - then the head and giant dorsal and sweeping tail. As the ogre passed, the eye of the man-eater focused on his next feast, then disappeared into the depths.

Ziad froze, paralyzed by fear - shocked by the immensity of the creature.

"This fucker is going to eat me alive." The words rolled off his bloodied tongue.

Ziad didn't see the creature coming up from the depths until the final seconds. A gaping mouth with multiple rows of serrated teeth engulfed his legs, swallowing him up to his waist. Snapping his jaws together, the behemoth shook his massive head from side to side - severing Ziad's body in half.

Hormones roared into Ziad's brain nullifying all sense of pain. With his intestines dangling from his abdomen like a string of sausages, and blood streaming from his eviscerated bowels, he envisioned the blessings that Allah had promised. As the giant predator faded into the darkness, Ziad realized the end was only seconds away.

"Come on! Finish me. Send me to my palace of pleasure."

The king of all man-eaters made a full turn and attacked from behind. With one crushing bite, Ziad's left shoulder, arm, and left half of his chest disappeared down the throat of the great white, leaving Ziad's head and what remained of his carcass bobbing up and down in blood-tinted swells.

****

Wednesday, 6:00 AM (0600 hours)

Hovering near the surface, the white mass of vapor moved with the wind, a gentle offshore breeze pushing westward.

Djinni had motored outside the perimeter of the restricted zone scanning the surface of the ocean for the Chechen divers. Drenched by the wet haze and confused as to his location, he looked at his GPS. The numbers were meaningless without landmarks.

"Ziad!" he called out. "Khalid, are you out there? Talk to me!" He was lost in a sea of fog - billions of microscopic droplets absorbed his screams until they too were lost in the fog.

Even the swells were confused - some rolled in from the left, others from the right - the next one a mirror image of its predecessor.

"Trust your instruments," he mumbled, gripping his GPS. "That's the only way out of this gloomy haze."

He reversed his course to return to Hakeem. Several minutes later, his GPS indicated he was back to where he had left him, but Hakeem was nowhere in sight.

"Hakeem! Hakeem!" he called out. "Hakeem! talk to me! Where are you?"

The mysterious mist swallowed his exhortations.

****

Wednesday, 9:45 AM (0945 hours)

Waiting impatiently for his shift break, control room operator Alvo (Big Al) Smith finished the last of his cold coffee and glanced over the expansive control panel. Colored lines traced the distribution schematics of the Ortega power plant. Red lines for electrical circuits, blue for hydraulics, green for cooling water, brown for steam, and so on.

The control panel was covered with hundreds of LED lights indicating the current status of assorted valves, sub-systems, and machinery: green lights for on, red lights for off, yellow lights for maintenance needed, flashing yellow lights for an emergency.

Big Al and his drinking buddy Lou often arrived for work feeling the effects of a two a.m. "last call for alcohol" at Dolly's Topless Saloon.

Here, in the privacy of the control room, Big Al and his pal quickly fell asleep.

"Hey, Lou. Wake up. I gotta pee. Watch the panel for me, will ya."

Lifting his head from his arm and opening his eyes, Lou replied, "Yeah, sure, man," then leaned back in his chair, closed his eyes and returned to his fantasies.

When he returned to his seat at the control panel, Big Al noticed the yellow flashing light indicating some sort of malfunction with the rotating biological intervention screen.

"Jesus Christ. I wonder how long this light has been blinking. Lou, Lou. Wake up. We've got a problem in the pump room. Go check it out."

"Piss off. If it's so important, you check it out. The last time this happened it was a dead seal. I can't move. God damn that Suzy Teez. She had some knockers. Been thinking about them luscious goodies all night."

"Okay, man. But you owe me one."

Big Al walked down the hall and took the elevator down three stories to the pump room. As he approached the rotating biological intervention screen he pulled up short. There, hung up in the chain link mesh, was the body of a diver. As a former soldier, he was shocked but not panicked. He picked up the phone and dialed the shift security supervisor.

"Hey, there's a dead guy caught up in the intervention screen. Better get someone down here right away."

VIGILANCE

Wednesday, 11:35 AM (1135 hours)

"Allan, this fog could not have come at a worse time. Is there any way we can truck a couple of dolphins to Ortega? Brady and Pace could join them."

"That will take too much time. And we have no way of launching or communicating with them from the beach."

"We've got to get our first response team into the restricted zone immediately. Who knows, the plant may have already been breached."

"We can't land the helicopter or take the DSB in this soup."

"I've got an idea." Greg's mind was flying on overdrive. "The chopper can take off from here and deploy Adam and X-ray off the Ortega beach using the water slides. April can set up a *Songbook* station inside the helicopter with a transceiver trailing in the water. I assume the chopper can hover over the ocean in the fog?"

"My pilots can hover all right using high definition autopilot. However, landing is out of the question."

Greg turned to face April. There was a glint of optimism in his eyes. "Brady will jump from the helicopter with X-ray, swim ashore with his dive gear, DULAN communication system, and EOD tools. X-ray can swim up the pipeline to join Brady in the pump room. Adam can patrol the red zone. You can lower a *Songbook* transceiver from the helicopter to communicate with him. At least we'll have some assets on the clock."

"Brady is going to need help on the inside. I'll get Chief Pace to join him. He can keep in touch with Brady and X-ray from inside the pump room with his DULAN comm. system."

"Great. I've got to call the boss. He'll bring DHS and the Joint Chiefs up to speed."

****

"David, this is Greg Mason. We have a situation at the Ortega nuclear power plant."

"Give me the thirty-second version."

"Evidence of a terrorist attack is being accumulated as we speak - possible infiltration through the induction pipe. We assume the motive is to shut down the cooling pumps."

"What is your situation?"

"We're mobilizing all available assets, but Ortega is presently blanketed by a heavy fog."

Stratton's mind whirled. "I need to inform DHS and the Joint Chiefs. They'll want a regular update, so keep me informed. If this thing goes south, I need to know immediately."

"I'll be in touch as things progress." Greg and David hung up simultaneously.

****

Chief Pace directed the loading of Adam and X-ray into the dolphin holding tanks while Jake, the pilot, checked and double-checked his flight instruments and fired up the powerful turbojet engines of the Super Huey.

April, Brady, and Pace buckled up their shoulder harnesses and covered their ears with noise cancellation headsets muffling the high-pitched screams from the twin turbojets.

"Everybody locked in?" asked Jake over the intercom. "All

set," Brady replied. Turning to April, he pointed to his watch and shook his head.

Their trip to Ortega passed over the Silver Strand beach, past the iconic Hotel del Coronado, over North Island Naval Air Station, the nuclear submarine base at Point Loma, above the cliffs of La Jolla and the sandy beaches to the north.

****

Wednesday, 12:45 PM (1245 hours)

Djinni heard the roar of the approaching helicopter. The fog was slowly lifting and he knew he'd be spotted if he remained in the immediate area.

"Ziad and Khalid are probably dead. Hakeem is lost in the fog. The Americans are mobilizing. I'd better get away from the red zone." His head began to pound from the thought of being captured and tortured by the infidels. "I probably have enough power to travel five or six miles out to sea. Yeah, that's what I'll do - wait offshore until after dark. Tonight is a new moon - the darkest night of the month. There may still be some fog cover too. I will return after midnight. I must inform the Sheik my mission was successful - that Ortega is doomed and thousands of non-believers will perish."

He turned his kayak west and motored out to sea.

****

"Hey, you guys," shouted Jake. "We're on station. I'll drop the dolphins first, then Brady and Pace."

"What's our altitude?" asked Brady.

"Hovering at twenty feet, fifty yards outside the breakers."

"Roger."

[APRIL] Adam. Are you ready to jump into the ocean?

[ADAM] I am ready.

[APRIL] X-ray. Are you all set to jump?

[X-RAY] Yes.

"Okay, Jake. You can release the dolphins."

Jake pulled the release lever on holding tank number one. Adam slid head-first down the dolphin water slide into the water. He quickly swam away from the helicopter rotor wash as Jake released X-ray.

"Okay, Brady. Both dolphins in the water. It's your turn," ordered Jake.

"Roger that."

Dressed in his chemically heated hot water wetsuit, with the DULAN communication system and closed circuit diving equipment, Brady grasped his EOD tools and leaped into the water.

"Okay, Pace. You're next. Good luck."

Pace wore a standard wetsuit, facemask and fins. He gripped the composite case containing his DULAN communication system and slipped into the sea, descending a few feet below the prop wash. Upon surfacing, he raised his right thumb, then swam off toward the beach with Brady.

"I am lowering the *Songbook* transceiver," said April.

"Roger," replied Jake.

With the transceiver fully submerged, April initiated her communication with the dolphins.

[APRIL] Adam. How do you hear me?

[ADAM} I hear you good.

[APRIL] X-ray. Do you hear me?

[X-RAY] I hear you loud and clear.

[APRIL] X-ray. Swim into the pipe. Wait for Brady in the pump room.

[X-RAY] I am on my way. Tell Adam to watch out for great white sharks. Ortega is one of their favorite beaches.

[ADAM] Thank you X-ray.

[APRIL] Adam. Please search the restricted area for intruders. The terrorists may be in inflatable kayaks. X-ray says to watch out for great white sharks.

Adam swam a spiraling circular reconnaissance route. Using his acute echolocation capabilities, he swiftly determined his location relative to the induction pipeline and the La Jolla Trench. Off to his right, he detected X-ray heading for the entrance of the induction pipe. He then fixed on Brady and Pace, swimming through the surf. On the shoreline, Adam saw two security guards awaiting their arrival.

****

Wednesday, 1:40 PM (1340 hours)

The latest dolphin support boat (DSB) was considerably larger than the earlier versions. At forty-five feet, her jet pump propulsion units were powered by twin fifteen-hundred-horsepower turbo-diesel engines providing a top speed of fifty miles an hour. Four interconnecting dolphin holding tanks straddled the after deck where eight-hundred-pound dolphins could be deployed at five-second intervals using the water slide.

The wheel house held a large array of navigation and communication systems including a sonar station, night vision cameras, remote-controlled vehicle pilot station, and *Songbook* communication control, all with a clear view of the surrounding sea.

While their primary function was to support DARPA and Navy dolphin operations, the DSB was well equipped for combat operations against enemy air, land, or seaborne forces. Her specialized weapon systems consisted of a Butler-15 combat drone capable of carrying four Brimstone infrared homing missiles, or two MK-5 video-guided cluster bombs. On her bow boldly stood the US Navy's latest fast-gun, a twenty-millimeter tungsten-iridium Volcano Gatling gun. Capable of firing up to six thousand high-density rounds per minute, this weapon could take out enemy jet fighters, incoming missiles, or a hostile vessel three times her size.

Below deck were a spacious galley with seating for twelve,

captain's quarters, four guest cabins, and sleeping quarters for the six-man crew.

"You can store your personal items in the guest cabins. We'll be departing momentarily."

Greg walked up to Uno and scratched his rostrum. Uno and Luke quickly recognized Greg and struck up a lengthy sing-song of whistles. Greg reached into the bait bucket and gave each dolphin a sardine treat.

"Hi there, fellas. Are you ready for another mission?"

The dolphins tossed their heads up and down. Even though Greg's words were not translated into Dolphinese, they understood the gist of his question.

"Who's our *Songbook* operator today?" Greg asked the skipper.

"SEAL vet-tech first class Squires. He's one of April's students. Top-notch operator. That's him on the fantail."

Greg turned and waved. "Hey, Squires. I understand you're one of April's students?"

"Yes, sir. She's one fabulous teacher. Is she working with us on this operation?"

"She's in a helicopter."

"I understand things are getting pretty tense. I heard it might be some sort of a bomb inside the induction pipe."

"I don't know where you heard that, but please don't repeat it. It's classified. Damn rumors spread like smallpox so keep your opinions to yourself."

"Yes, sir."

Engaging the powerful engines, the coxswain slowly moved the DSB away from the pier.

Greg was dismayed at the lack of anti-terrorist vigilance and forethought by the Ortega security forces. Disgusted with the poor security, he looked at his friend Allan.

"We have a serious security problem in this country. Everyone seems to think we're immune. Nobody really cares.

Ortega security knew they had a possible breach *thirty-six hours ago.*"

Allan shrugged his shoulders. "Our complacency may be our doom."

The moment the DSB cleared the channel marker, her coxswain pushed the throttles to the limit sending the bow to a steep angle and a large rooster tail jettisoning from the transom. While the fog remained at Ortega, the sky was clear in San Diego.

"What's your plan, Lieutenant?" asked Greg as sea spray washed across his face.

"Weather permitting, we'll pick up April from the helicopter, then launch the dolphins at the southwest corner of the restricted zone. We'll head north over the La Jolla Trench to the northern corner, then dogleg a hundred feet to the east and return to the southern border. The dolphins will go where they please, following their instincts, investigating any extraneous acoustical or visual contacts. Squires will keep in touch with them as they cruise up and down the restricted zone. Or, if you wish, April can do it."

"I believe she'll want the job once she arrives onboard."

"No problem. Hey, Squires, your teacher will soon be coming aboard. She wants your job," Lewis chuckled.

"Glad to have her. She's the best."

EOD: EXPLOSIVE ORDNANCE DISPOSAL

Wednesday 1:45 PM (1345 hours)

Located thirty feet below sea level, the Ortega pump room hummed with a life of its own. The rotating biological intervention screen stood several feet forward of the water pumps. It's twenty-foot-wide chain-link metal screen clickety-clanked over a hydraulic drive gear trapping stray fish, crabs, jellyfish, kelp, or debris that might otherwise become sucked into the cooling pumps.

To the right of the rotating screen was a passageway leading to the reservoir. Here, Pace could set up his *Songbook* equipment, Brady had direct access to the induction pipe and X-ray could surface for a breath of fresh air.

The Ortega nuclear power plant employs a once-through cooling system. Huge centrifugal cooling pumps, one for each of the two reactors, delivered cold seawater to maintain the appropriate reactor temperature. After passing through the reactor, the heated water was discharged back into the ocean.

Most nuclear reactor cooling pumps are installed vertically. The high-speed rotary impeller, shaft, and bearing assemblies are machined and balanced to extremely tight tolerances. Any foreign material, particularly sand, rocks, or suspended metal such as steel or aluminum cans, may cause these pumps to freeze. Without adequate cooling, residual heat from the nuclear fission process would reach the meltdown temperature within a few hours.

****

When Brady and Pace arrived, X-ray whistled and chirped to get Brady's attention. Brady and Pace were momentarily distracted by the sight of the body of a dead diver lying face-up on the deck of the pump room. His bloodied remains had been severely mangled by the rotating intervention screen.

Richard Winslow stood next to the dead terrorist, arms folded over his chest.

Pointing to the deceased diver, Brady yelled to Winslow, "We'll talk about this goon later. Right now, I've got to speak with X-ray. He's got something important to tell me."

The SEALs quickly set up their DULAN communication systems while X-ray anxiously waited to communicate his findings.

[BRADY] Hello X-ray. What's up?

[X-RAY] There is a linear shape charge in the induction pipe.

[BRADY] That is very bad news. Where is the bomb located?

[X-RAY] Four hundred feet from the pump room. It is buried below the surf zone. It is attached to the pipe with magnets.

[BRADY] Have you been able to see inside and determine the design?

[X-RAY] The explosive charge forms a square three feet on each side. The detonator assembly has at least three triggers. One is a mercury level switch. The second is a time pencil. The third is an electromagnetic contact bridge. It has a glowing flashlight bulb in the circuit. I need more time to see if there are more triggers.

[BRADY] How much time do we have?

[X-RAY] I do not know. The time pencil was labeled twenty-four hours but we don't know when it was initiated.

[BRADY] Twenty-four hour time pencils are unreliable. They often detonate much sooner.

[X-RAY] Then we must hurry.

[BRADY} Yes. What else can you tell me about this device?

[X-RAY] The mercury level switch is designed to prevent removal. Any movement over ten degrees in any direction will cause it to detonate.

[X-RAY] Hurry. You need to see this. Bring your tools. There are magnets in place to attach safety ropes to the pipe. You will need a couple of ropes with carabiner clips.

[BRADY] Give me a couple of minutes.

Brady gave Winslow a haunting glance. "Sorry, Winslow. We've got a huge problem. X-ray and I have a life or death situation to deal with - your life and mine."

"Anything I can do to help?"

"Yeah. Call the Dana Point dive center. Get me a couple of chemical heater cartridges for my hot water wetsuit. I brought an extra one with me, but they're only good for a couple of hours."

Brady grabbed his EOD tool kit and submerged.

"Excuse me, sir," barked Pace, looking at Winslow. "I've got to have some room. Why don't you go make that call? We've got work to do." Pace gave Winslow his infamous "don't fuck with me" scowl.

[BRADY] X-ray. Are you ready to travel to the bomb site?

[X-RAY] All set. Take a grip on my dorsal fin. I will tow you to the bomb. The current is too strong for you to swim upstream.

[BRADY] Pace. Are you ready?

[PACE] All set. Good luck. Let me know when you need anything.

[X-RAY] I'll deliver tools to Brady.

[BRADY] Thanks X-ray. No telling how long it will take to disarm this brainteaser.

X-ray used his powerful tail flukes to tow Brady to the bomb site. Like a wild salmon treading water in a roaring mountain stream, X-ray swam against the incoming current while Brady hung onto his dorsal fin with one hand and attached two safety lines to the overhead magnets with the other hand.

[BRADY] Okay, guys. I'm locked into position facing the bomb. Wish me luck.

[PACE] How bad is the current?

[BRADY] Workable. It was nice of the terrorists to leave these magnets.

Brady began to inspect the bomb, searching for clues as to how it was designed - and more significantly - the pathway to disarmament.

****

"April," Jake shouted. "You have a call on channel two. It's Greg."

"Hi, what's up?"

"Allan and I are on our way to you in the DSB. I just got off the phone with Pace. X-ray found a bomb inside the induction pipe!"

April gasped. Then took a long, deep breath. "Fuck." There was no other word to describe her angst.

"Yeah, that's what I said. But wait, there's more. The body of one of the terrorists was discovered caught up in the rotating biological intervention screen along with his propulsion unit. He was torn up pretty badly. Winslow called the FBI and DHS folks to take charge of his body. Maybe they'll get a clue or two."

"I sure hope so."

"Listen, Brady and X-ray are in the pipe working on this thing as we speak. Brady said this is a complicated design, not easily disarmed. Pace is assisting them from the pump room. You're probably running low on fuel. You can transfer to the DSB in the chairlift as soon as we arrive. Has Adam found anything?"

"No. We're still socked in with fog, but it is lifting. God, I hope Brady and X-ray can disarm this bomb. Where exactly did they place it?"

"Under the surf zone. These guys are no dummies. It looks like they wanted to flood the pipe and pumps with sand. That would definitely trash the impellers and kill the source of cooling water."

"My God. This is frightening. What is this world coming to?"

"I love you. Stay safe. I'll keep you posted. Call me if you have any news."

"I love you too. Goodbye."

****

Wednesday 2:05 PM (1405 hours)

[ADAM] April. I found the upper body of a diver. He was wearing pieces of a Russian diving system.

[APRIL] What do you mean pieces of a Russian diving system?

[ADAM] He is missing his legs and his stomach and a large section of his chest.

[APRI] Where did you find the remains?

[ADAM] About three hundred yards west of the red zone. It was a great white.

[APRIL] Good work Adam. Brady and X-ray found a dead diver too. He was tangled up in the biological intervention screen.

[ADAM] Is Ortega going to have a nuclear meltdown?

April was shocked to discover Adam had somehow figured out the full scope of the emergency.

[APRIL] I don't know. I certainly hope not.

[ADAM] Shall I continue my mission?

[APRIL] Yes. Keep looking. There may be more terrorists. Greg is aboard the DSB. He will be here soon. The fog has made it impossible for us humans to see. The terrorists may be in small boats with a weak acoustic signature.

[ADAM] I will do my best.

****

140

Greg and Allan sat in the DSB galley contemplating the gravity of their predicament when Lieutenant Lewis approached. "Greg, April is on the horn. She has an urgent message for you."

Greg slapped his palm on the table and dashed off to the radio room, haunted by imaginings of a world gone mad - his beautiful wife April in harm's way.

"Hi, April. What's up?"

"Adam found another dead diver. Well, not exactly. He found a portion of him drifting in the current outside the restricted zone. He was wearing what was left of a Russian oxygen re-breather. He's probably been dead for several hours."

HAKEEM'S BUMBLEBEE

Wednesday, 2:25 PM (1425 hours)

The glow from the sun began to penetrate the mist. Hakeem had not seen Djinni for several hours and he had no idea where the current had propelled him. To his delight, off in the distance, Hakeem saw the dark outline of the power plant.

Rejuvenated by the sight of Ortega, Hakeem decided to fulfill his jihad. He didn't need Djinni to accomplish his mission. His five-pound weapon of mass destruction - his deadly bumblebee - would fulfill his destiny. He just needed to get closer to his target - within range of his remote control unit.

"Execute the plan," he declared.

Hakeem engaged the electric motor and quietly propelled his inflatable toward Ortega. Moments later, he passed the barnacle-encrusted buoy marking the outer perimeter of the restricted zone. Off in the distance, he heard the sound of a helicopter.

"Now," he whispered. "Now is the time." He was well inside the red zone when he cut the power to his motor and drifted silently across the glassy swells. The fog had lifted several feet above the sea providing a partial view of the power plant rising up from the beach like a mysterious alien temple. To the left stood the storage site where dozens of nuclear waste storage canisters sat upright - their thin metal tops exposed to the elements. He readied the drone, double-checked the camera and controls and set the detonator for ten seconds after contact.

****

[ADAM] April. I have a contact entering the restricted zone. I will investigate and advise.

[APRIL] What is the bearing and range?

[ADAM] Bearing one eighty-eight. Range four hundred yards.

[April] Got it. We are on our way. Be careful.

Adam rushed to intercept the contact. As he closed the distance, the image of a man in an inflatable kayak came into focus. Adam stopped and raised his body several feet into the air to get a better view of the target.

[ADAM] It is an inflatable kayak with one human. He is heading closer to Ortega. What shall I do?

[APRIL] Intimidate the human. Try to get him to retreat. Do not wait for us. Escalate your response to nullify the threat if he does not retreat.

[ADAM] Thank you.

Adam raced toward the kayak, forcefully ramming it with his rostrum. Hakeem lost his balance and stumbled back from the impact. Hakeem lifted his head above the starboard side inflation tube and came face to face with Adam displaying his two-inch-long conical teeth while emitting an array of painful, high-frequency squeals.

Startled, Hakeem struggled to his knees and scrambled toward the bow.

"Fuck off! Go away!" Hakeem shouted, waving his arms above his head.

Shaking his rostrum from side to side, Adam let loose another volley of high-pitched squeals.

"Get away from me!" Hakeem screamed.

Using his powerful flukes, Adam rose up, his head and pectorals high above the side of the kayak. Upon seeing the drone and remote controller, he slid back and dove deep.

[ADAM] The man in the kayak has a remote-controlled drone. A small bomb and camera are attached to it.

[APRIL] Do not wait for us. Nullify the threat now.

[ADAM] I will nullify the threat.

As much as April detested the thought of harming another human being, she knew it was her duty to protect America from terrorists by any possible means.

Adam charged the kayak, jumping high above Hakeem to the opposite side of the inflatable. His eight-hundred-pound body landed on his flank sending a large wave over the kayak. Hakeem thrashed about the floor of his kayak in a foot of water.

"Fucking dolphin. Are you crazy?" The noise of the approaching helicopter set Hakeem into a panic.

Grasping the remote control, he applied power to the drone and pulled back on the joystick. The drone climbed a few feet above the surface of the water and hovered against the fog while Hakeem programmed the flight path. Setting a course for the dry storage area, he would have preferred flying higher, but he needed to keep the drone in view until his target appeared on his video monitor.

Adam raced ahead of the drone and dove deep to build up his momentum. His timing was precise. He accelerated to attack speed, leaped high into the air and rammed his rostrum into the drone, destroying one of the four battery-powered motors.

Spinning wildly out of control, the drone rolled over and crashed into the ocean. Adam quickly turned his attention to Hakeem and commenced his attack.

Suddenly, Adam felt a harmless shockwave from an underwater explosion. The shaped charge obliterated Hakeem's drone and left a foot-deep hole in the sandy bottom.

Powering up his kayak, Hakeem headed out to sea

screaming, "Allahu Akbar."

Adam didn't hesitate. He sprinted forward until he was head to head with the terrorist. There was no stopping the awesome power and determination of the charging cetacean.

Adam wrapped his gaping jaws around the port inflation tube ripping a long gash down her side. He then dove under the kayak and opened a similar gash in the starboard tube.

Hakeem had long ago abandoned the thought of using his *shahid* grenade and had tossed it into the sea. Knowing he was doomed in a rapidly sinking kayak, Hakeem wrapped the anchor line around his ankles, tied an overhand knot and prepared to jump.

From the helicopter, April saw Hakeem preparing to commit suicide.

"Don't do it!" she screamed. The roar of the chopper masked her plea.

"Allahu Akbar!" Hakeem shouted. Holding the anchor high above his head, he leaped into the sea.

"He's gone," asserted April. "My God. He killed himself."

"We'll never recover his body. He's over the La Jolla Trench," said Jake.

Numbed by thoughts of receiving Allah's seven blessings, Hakeem didn't feel the cold water enveloping his body - it was, in his mind, a prelude to the welcome he would soon embrace in the kingdom of Allah.

As he plunged deeper into the cavernous trench, he felt the pain of bursting eardrums, followed seconds later by a desperate urge to breathe. Hakeem forcefully expelled the last of his air… and ended his life with a lungful of seawater.

TICK-TOCK-TICK

Wednesday, 3:50 PM (1550 hours)
April looked down from the helicopter while it hovered steadily above the DSB. The crew had transferred her communication equipment and it was time for her to transfer from the helicopter to the dolphin support boat.

April sang out, trying her best to be heard over the roar of the helicopter. "Harness secured." She re-checked her safety harness around her waist and shoulders. "Okay, Jake. I'm all set."

"Roger. Good luck, April. We'll be rooting for you and your dolphins to get those bastards before they do any damage."

"Thanks for the ride, Jake."

Jake engaged the winch while the boat crew held the safety line to keep her from oscillating. April shuffled out of the helicopter and drifted away from the fuselage while she slowly descended to the deck of the DSB. The instant she touched down, Jake let the winch free-spool allowing the crew to release April from the harness.

Jake made a slow turn away from the DSB and headed back to Camp Pendleton to refuel.

"Hello, Squires. Thanks for the welcoming party. Where's Greg?"

"He's in the galley with Allan. They've been on the phone to DC since we left."

April rushed into the galley and gave Greg a hug.

"We've got a major challenge on our hands. Brady is still trying to figure out how to dismantle this complex bomb. X-ray has been a tremendous help - but so far he has not been able to get inside the device." Perspiration rolled down Greg's temples.

April shook her head in dismay. "What else can we do? There must be a way to disarm this thing. So many lives are at stake."

"Brady is the best. If anyone can do it - Brady can," said Allan confidently.

"I'm going to put Uno and Luke in the water to help Adam. There may be more terrorists in the area."

"Squires will give you a hand," said Greg.

April rushed to the *Songbook* com station to brief Uno and Luke.

[APRIL] Hello Uno and Luke.

[UNO] Greetings April. It's nice to see you.

[LUKE] Hello April.

[APRIL] Adam is in the water. He found a dead terrorist and scared another into committing suicide. There may be more bad guys in the area and he needs your help finding them.

[UNO] That is a simple mission.

[APRIL] One of them has a black patch over one eye. He is probably in an inflatable kayak.

[LUKE] What shall we do if we find him?

[APRIL] Greg will let us know.

****

Wednesday, 6:45 PM (1845 hours)

[BRADY] There are some challenging features in this bomb design. I cannot find any way inside. I think the box is laser-welded titanium.

147

[X-RAY] Let me have another look.

X-ray touched his rostrum to the outside of the detonator box and began to raster scan across the surface.

[X-RAY] You are correct. The detonator box is titanium. You will need your laser to drill a hole large enough for the endoscope and a second hole for your tools. You will also need the hot tap assembly to keep the box from flooding.

[BRADY] Chief Pace. I need the laser driller, hot-tap assembly, and endoscope. X-ray is on his way to pick them up.

X-ray could hold his breath underwater for about ten minutes. When in need of oxygen or to retrieve special tools for Brady, he rushed back to the pump room. His round trip took less than a minute.

[X-RAY] Drill from the bottom. Set the hot tap assembly for ten pounds per square inch of positive pressure. It is very important to keep water from entering the detonator box. It could complete the electrical circuit.

[BRADY] Right. I'm going to drill a small hole near the bottom. Is there a preferred location?

[X-RAY] Either of the two nearest corners.

Brady moved the hot tap assembly and focusing optics into position and dialed up the pulse profile on the diode laser power supply.

[BRADY] Setting laser profile to eighty nanoseconds, three joules at one kilohertz. I'm focusing a two-micron spot with a six-millimeter stand-off. This should give us a four- millimeter hole in about sixty seconds.

Brady commenced firing the laser. Microscopic fragments of titanium flew off the surface.

[BRADY] Penetration complete. Raising interior pressure to fifteen psi. Now inserting endoscope.

[PACE] Take it easy. Look out for any water seepage.

[BRADY] Yeah, I know. Water and electricity don't mix.

[BRADY] I've got light. The flashlight bulb is on. That means the electromagnet contact bridge is secure until the battery dies.

Brady held his breathing in check while maneuvering the endoscope around the interior of the detonator box, exercising extreme caution while scanning the interior.

[BRADY] I have the time pencil in view. It's a standard design. Six inches long. You're right X-ray. It's labeled twenty-four hours. But we don't know when the time started. It could have been initiated yesterday or early this morning.

[X-RAY] Odds are the time pencil goes off before the electromagnetic contact. Do not be concerned about the mercury switch. It can be disarmed last. Your priority is the time pencil followed by the electromagnetic contact.

{BRADY] You are a genius X-ray. I am going to need another hole directly opposite the time pencil.

Brady removed the fiber optic light and retrieved the laser and hot-tap assembly.

[BRADY] Increasing the internal pressure to twenty psi. Placing the second hole thirty millimeters above the first. Same laser parameters. Here we go.

[BRADY] Pace. We have another hole. Time to defuse the time pencil.

[PACE] What do you need?

[BRADY] The quick-set epoxy injector. I am sending X-ray to pick it up.

Brady positioned himself in a more comfortable position. He tightened the safety lines and took several deep breaths, focusing on the task at hand, lowering his heart rate. This procedure reminded him of taking a sniper shot at fifteen hundred yards. It was all about breathing, relaxing, and concentrating on the target.

Several wrenching seconds ticked by as Brady finalized his strategy. Even the slightest mistake, too much pressure, a misaligned laser beam, or minuscule vibration could cause the bomb to detonate. Brady was nervous. He had never done this procedure before. But he knew how to control his emotions and keep a steady hand.

[BRADY] Pace please record these next few steps. I would not want the next EOD guy to find out the hard way this maneuver would be his last. First, I will drill a hole in the time pencil case big enough to insert the quick-set epoxy nozzle. Give me a second to figure out the right location. This has to be perfect. If I accidentally make contact with the trip wire it will probably break. It is already damaged from the acid and will not take much of a tap to separate. X-ray and I will be covered with tons of sand in a matter of seconds. The cooling pumps will die a few minutes later. That pretty much sums it up.

[PACE] Got it. Stay cool.

Using the endoscope to observe his movements, Brady positioned the laser drill at an upward angle a couple of millimeters above the centerline of the time pencil.

[BRADY] Damn. I cannot see shit. I am working blind.

He paused to collect himself.

[PACE] Stay calm. Follow your instincts.

Brady placed the focusing optics near the top of the time pencil and pulled the trigger. Sparks flew off from the thin brass case. With a short popping sound, he stopped and slowly backed off the laser leaving a small hole near the top of the time pencil.

[BRADY] We have a hole. Okay. Now we must secure the trip wire and insulate the contacts.

Brady continued talking aloud - not to Chief Pace or X-ray - but to keep his mind focused on the precise sequence of the delicate defusing process and make an audio record of his actions. At this stage of the operation, it was more like open heart surgery - one false move, one little hiccup would be a death sentence - not for Brady and X-ray - but for tens of thousands.

[BRADY] Taking hold of the quick-set epoxy injector, he looked into the endoscope. With the utmost care, he guided the tip into the hole. Steadying his hand, he squeezed the trigger, releasing a few cubic centimeters of liquid epoxy and catalyst. The instant he saw excess epoxy oozing from the hole, he stopped. As he removed the injector he mentally counted back from sixty…fifty-nine…fifty-eight…

[BRADY] Hooyah! We have secured the time pencil.

[PACE] Can you cut the battery wires now?

[BRADY] Not yet. I must insulate the contacts below the electromagnet.

[X-RAY] The bulb is still bright. The battery is good for another hour.

[BRADY] We have some breathing room, but I am a little woozy and need something to eat. Come on X-ray. We are almost done. Let us disable the electromagnetic switch. It will only take a few minutes.

[X-RAY] I am with you all the way.

[BRADY] You are one fine friend, X-ray. And one very smart dolphin.

Peering into the endoscope, Brady located electrical contact pins a few millimeters apart. Directly above the contacts, an electromagnet held a thin steel bridge plate. This type of switch was most often used as a booby trap. If the battery wires are cut or the battery dies, the bridge plate falls across the contacts, thereby completing the circuit and detonating the bomb. It was a simple design - one that many experienced EOD men had mistakenly believed could be disarmed by cutting the wires to the battery.

[BRADY] I am positioning the tip of the epoxy injector over the two contacts. Okay, I am now releasing quick-set epoxy on top of the contacts.

[BRADY] Hooyah! Both contacts are insulated. Two down, one to go. What do you think X-ray? Is there anything unusual about this mercury switch?”

[X-RAY] Let me have another look inside. I have an idea but I need to check on something first.

Brady moved aside to provide X-ray with the best possible viewing angle.

X-ray swam around to the back side of the detonator box and scanned the interior.

[X-RAY] I thought so.

[BRADY] You thought what?

[X-RAY] There is a counterbalance on the back side and another battery. Both are obscured by the mercury switch. The counterbalance is connected to a leaf spring. It weighs a few grams more than the mercury. We cannot remove the mercury. It will trigger the counterbalance and the bomb will explode.

[BRADY] I have never seen anything like this before. These ISIS bastards are becoming masters at this bomb making business. You and I need to think on this one. Shit. I am really puzzled. What shall I do?

Unable to determine the facts himself, Brady was miffed at being outmatched by the terrorists and upstaged by his dolphin partner.

[X-RAY] Lock the mercury in place.

[BRADY] What do you mean?

[X-RAY] Cover the mercury with quick-set epoxy. Encapsulate it. Lock it up. Keep it from moving like a liquid. That will isolate the counterbalance feature.

[BRADY] Brilliant X-ray. Brilliant.

Brady drilled a small hole in the top of the mercury switch, inserted the epoxy nozzle and injected a large volume of quick-set epoxy on top of the liquid mercury. After removing the nozzle, he watched the second hand on his Rolex complete a full circle.

****

Wednesday, 8:50 PM (2050 hours)

[BRADY] X-ray and I are coming out. Ask Winslow to call in the agents from DHS and FBI. We have got a present for them.

Upon surfacing, Brady tossed the disassembled sections of

the linear shape charge onto the deck. Everyone instinctively jumped back.

Slightly waterlogged and dead tired, he looked at his watch. It was ten minutes to nine in the evening. It had taken eight hours of surgical precision to defuse the bomb.

"There ya go. One disarmed boogeyman. Don't fret over it. The detonator is as benign as a tennis ball."

"My God, man. You did it. You disarmed it. Congratulations. You'll get a medal for this." Richard was absolutely giddy with relief.

"Give the medal to X-ray. He did the analytics."

****

Greg had just taken a sip of his fifth cup of coffee when the call came in.

"Greg, this is Winslow. They did it! Brady and X-ray disarmed the bomb!"

"Oh, my God! That is fabulous news. Wow! Exceptional! Brilliant!"

Winslow continued. "They were underwater for about eight hours. It was a delicate situation for much of the time. Those bastards threw everything in the booby trap book at them, but they pulled it off. DHS packaged it up and hauled it off for analysis."

"I'm at a loss for words right now. Give me a moment to digest this remarkable development. Whew!" Greg took a few deep breaths and refocused on the last piece of business.

"At least one terrorist is still at large. We've got our dolphins in the water. If he's anywhere near Ortega, they'll find him."

Greg hung up and rushed onto the deck of the DSB - tears of salvation flooded his eyes.

"April, they did it. Brady and X-ray disarmed the bomb. Ortega is secure."

April jumped up and down wrapping her arms around

Greg and kissing him wildly about the face and mouth. "That is awesome news. Thank you, Lord." April looked up to the heavens.

"What's happening up here? Any sign of our one-eyed jihadist?" Greg inquired.

"Our dolphins are working on it."

"We've got to nullify that son-of-a-bitch!"

MARTYRDOM

Thursday, 1:30 AM (0130 hours)

It was a moonless night; some call it a new moon. Djinni had been awake for almost three days. Emotionally drained, he groaned and shook some sense of reality into his head.

With lots of luck and a little ingenuity, Djinni had managed to remain out of sight, first because of the heavy fog and later by motoring several miles out to sea. He was delighted with his decision to use inflatable kayaks - invisible to any man-made sonar - stealthy as a leopard.

But it was well past the time his bomb should have exploded, and that gave him grave concern. Maybe it had detonated but the sound was muffled. Of one thing he was certain: nobody could disarm it - no way - not one of his masterpieces.

"I've got to know what's happening. Allah must know of my triumph over the infidels." The suspense drove Djinni far beyond his keen sense of danger. Casting all his intuitive notions aside, he powered up the outboard motor and pointed the bow toward Ortega.

He had traveled less than a mile when his battery suddenly died. He could clearly see the lights of Ortega - its giant pair of breast-shaped containment vessels reaching far above the ground, a bright red navigation light twinkling atop each nipple

"Fucking battery - didn't give me any warning - just up and quit. Guess I'll have to paddle." Djinni liked to talk to himself; it seemed to calm his nerves to verbalize his ups and downs. He picked up the paddle and set a steady pace toward Ortega.

****

[ADAM] April, I heard an electric outboard motor bearing 250 degrees at six thousand yards. It was heading toward the restricted zone but suddenly stopped.

[APRIL] That must be our man. Please approach the target with caution.

[ADAM] I am on my way.

[UNO] I will follow Adam.

[LUKE] I heard the contact too. I will join Adam and Uno.

[ADAM] We are headed toward the contact. Lights out. Silent mode.

"Greg!" April bellowed into the galley. "We have a hit. Grab a couple of night vision binoculars and come topside."

****

As he approached the restricted zone, Djinni's obsession intensified. Would Allah be pleased? Even if he failed, he would die trying. Of that, there was no doubt. But would he be accepted into Allah's promised land? Would he be honored and revered as the most courageous and faithful martyr of all time? Surely Allah would bestow upon him all seven of his well-deserved blessings.

[ADAM] April. I see one man with an eye patch in an inflatable kayak. He's paddling toward the restricted zone.

[APRIL] Dolphins move in close. Make an audio distraction to shield the DSB.

****

Djinni heard Adam approach his kayak, then stop a few meters from his port side and begin to whistle and chirp with a bewildering cacophony.

Shining his flashlight on Adam, Djinni visualized an omen. "You must be a messenger from Allah." Adam continued his incessant chattering.

Suddenly Uno and Luke appeared next to Adam. To Djinni's delight, they immediately joined Adam emitting a loud and unrelenting stream of whistles, chirps, and squeaks.

"Praise Allah, for he has not forsaken me. Such a warm greeting he has bestowed upon me. Surely my bomb has exploded. Why else would Allah send three emissaries to congratulate me with songs of praise and redemption?"

As he paddled closer to the restricted zone, the dolphins continued their ruckus.

"I can see the kayak and Mr. One-eye!" exclaimed Greg peering through his night vision binoculars.

"Yeah, I've got him too," said Allan. "Skipper, reduce power. Everyone quiet. Drift in closer and then light him up with the high beams."

Djinni continued to mistakenly believe the dolphins were singing songs of gratitude and glory, when in fact, they were purposefully drowning out the sound of the DSB.

Suddenly, Djinni was blinded by the high-intensity searchlight illuminating his body like a rock star making his grandiose entrance at the London Palladium.

"Stop! You are under arrest. Raise your arms. Place your hands behind your head and lock your fingers," Allan shouted over the bullhorn.

Djinni was momentarily paralyzed. His mind was not prepared to see an American warship filled with armed infidels. He quickly realized he'd been duped by a trio of singing dolphins.

"Fucking infidels!" Djinni screamed as his instincts took control of his actions.

He reached into his pocket and pulled out his *shahid* grenade.

"Do not move. Raise your hands above your head!" Allan yelled over the bullhorn.

Djinni looked upon the DSB with the face of a disdainful demon. With one arm in the air and his one eye on Greg and April, Djinni flipped open the top with his thumb.

"Stop what you're doing. Put both arms behind your head," Allan bellowed.

Djinni twisted the numbered barrels to 666, then paused, waiting for the DSB to drift closer.

"He's got a grenade!" Greg shouted. "Take cover!"

Everyone dove for the nearest defensive location.

Sensing the impending hazard, the dolphins quickly ducked beneath the surface.

Djinni pushed the red button.

Milliseconds later, bits and pieces of body parts blew high into the hereafter.

"Holy shit!" Allan was appalled. "He just blew himself up. Jesus Christ. Look, there's nothing left - blood and guts every-where - and a few pieces of a shredded kayak."

"April, are you okay?" asked Greg.

"I never imagined I'd witness a martyr. I'm covered with blood and tissue, but I'm fine."

[APRIL] Dolphins are you okay?

[ADAM} Yes. Did the terrorist commit suicide?

[APRIL] Yes. He was a very bad man. He wanted to kill thousands of people.

[UNO] Then he deserved to die.

[LUKE] He was an evil person.

"I believe that he was the last one - the leader," said Allan.

"Let's recover our dolphins and head for home," said April.

"Yeah. Let's go home." Greg gave April a kiss on the cheek. "We got the last of the terrorists. I've got to call David with the good news."

"Who was this guy?" asked Allan.

"Nobody seems to have any information on him," replied Greg.

"We certainly have enough of whoever he was for a DNA test," retorted Allan.

AN EYE FOR AN EYE

"So you and April are headed back home. Thanks for your help - both of you - and especially your dolphins."

"Well, Allan, what can I say except this has been the mother of all cliffhangers - one hell of an adventure."

"Yeah, maybe Hollywood will do a movie based on this epic saga. I bet it would be a real blockbuster."

"What a horrendous operation. Your team did a commendable job. Jake, your helicopter pilot, was amazing. He hovered for hours - almost ran out of fuel. That was very impressive. And those dolphin water slides - send me the plans and specs. I'll have our machine shop fabricate a couple of them. I'm sure Adam, Uno, and Luke will tell their Cape Canaveral companions how much fun they had sliding from a helicopter."

"Adam is the best. I know he's getting up there in years, but he's fearless."

"X-ray and Brady had the toughest assignment. They deserve special recognition for their heroic effort. Put in the paperwork. I'll sign off and pass it up the chain of command."

"Yeah, our dolphins and teammates took it all in stride. It's not just a job - it's an adventure. Isn't that some kind of motto?" Allan jested.

"Listen, you and Felicia need to come visit us in Florida

sometime. We've got some great beaches, warm water, and fantastic scuba diving. You and I can count the fish while the girls go shopping. How's that sound?"

"I'd love it and so would Felicia."

"April and I want to hear more about Felicia's plan to use our dolphins to warn wild cetaceans about dangerous migratory routes. There are still some crazies out there who have no respect for these magnanimous partners of ours."

"Hey, before I forget, I've got a present for you." Allan retrieved a small box from his desk. Handing it to Greg, he said, "It's a little memento from the terrorists. You know, those jihadists who are now wandering around some bleak desert landscape looking for their bevy of virgins. Open it up. If you don't like it, well, maybe I'll keep it for myself."

Greg shook the box while holding it up to his ear. "Sounds like a golf ball."

"Maybe. Maybe not. I'd say it's more of a collectible - something to pass on to your grandkids. It's got an exciting history. Go on. Open it."

Greg peeled back the foil wrapping and lifted the lid.

"What the… Jesus, it's a glass eye!"

"Yeah. I found it in the DSB after our one-eyed terrorist blew himself to smithereens. I had it sterilized and polished up nice and shiny just for you."

Greg held it between his thumb and index finger, twirling it in the sunlight, mesmerized by the thought this glass eye belonged to one of the most sinister and dangerous jihadist leaders ever to inhabit the planet. Or did it?

"Allan, this is kinda sick - damn thing staring back at me. I don't know about this. I appreciate the gift, but I've got nowhere to put it. It really is kinda morbid - damn thing keeps on looking at me. It's really creepy."

"Just think of all the idioms you can use when you show it to your friends."

"What idioms?"

"You know. As far as the *eye* can see. Beauty is in the *eye* of the beholder. Keep your *eye* on the ball."

Greg began to chuckle. "Stop, stop. I can't take any more."

"Aw. Come on, Greg. You must know someone with a roving *eye*. How about a jaundiced *eye*?"

Greg doubled up with laughter. "Please, Allan. No more."

Mulling over the recent events, both men gazed into the steel gray eye and snickered.

Allan had the last word. "Well, now that you mention it, maybe it is a bit creepy - maybe it isn't. It depends on how you look at it."

TAKE A PEEK .....

SAMPLE CHAPTERS FROM
TWO OF CRAIG'S OTHER BOOKS

Navy SEAL

DOLPHINS
IN
VIETNAM

———

NO LIFEGUARD ON DUTY
Legacy of a Navy SEAL

Navy SEAL
DOLPHINS
IN
VIETNAM

Synopsis

1972: South Vietnam: When a Chicago drug dealer gets involved in the heroin distribution business during the Vietnam War, he soon discovers he's no match for Commander (SEAL) Steve Mason and his Alpha Team dolphins. Using musical instructions and graphics, the dolphins must disable the cartel vessels and prevent 200 kilos of heroin from reaching American soldiers.

SUICIDE SAPPER DIVERS

It was October in South Vietnam - the wettest month of the year. A heavy downpour blurred the colorful lights of Da Nang and the sea-lane approaches to the American Naval base.

It was a perfect night for sabotage.

Two motorized sampans cut their engines and drifted silently toward the Navy fuel docks. Aboard each boat, two North Vietnamese Army suicide sapper divers began to 'psych-up' for their midnight mission.

"Time to go," said the coxswain.

The divers secured their facemasks and rolled into the water with as little noise as possible. The lead diver set their compass heading for the Navy fuel tanker moored at the fuel docks. After establishing the correct compass course, both divers slipped below the surface of the tepid water. Each man carried an explosive package designed to sink a US Navy fuel oil tanker.

The leader held the navigation board with both hands. It contained an underwater compass, depth gauge and watch. His dive partner cradled a loaded spear gun across his left arm.

The enemy divers knew their mission was suicidal. But after months of brainwashing, demagoguery and demonizing of America by their North Vietnamese handlers they were prepared to sacrifice their lives on behalf of their cherished leader, Ho Chi

Minh - even if it meant using the suicide hand grenade clipped to their belt.

****

Aboard the Dolphin Support Boat (DSB), Navy SEAL Bucky Daniels squinted through the rain and gave the order to release his Alpha Team dolphins Abe and Tiki from their holding tanks.

"Launch Abe and Tiki," he shouted. "I'll give them the search order."

The DSB crewmen secured Abe to the launch cradle and lowered him gently into the sea. They repeated the procedure with Tiki while Bucky prepared to give them their assignment. Shortly, the dolphins were in the water - anxiously circling - waiting for instructions.

Bucky looked into the eyes of his dolphins and slapped his right palm against the hull of the DSB.

"Listen up!" Bucky slapped his right palm a second time drawing the dolphins to the side of the DSB.

Abe and Tiki lifted their heads above the water eagerly searching for Bucky's mission instructions. Each dolphin held a small inflatable buoy in their mouth.

"Search for enemy divers. Tag the enemy divers." Bucky raised his right arm high above his head, pointed his index finger to the sky and rotated his arm in a wide circular motion - like a calf roping cowboy twirling his lariat. "Search for enemy divers. Tag enemy divers. Go now!" With his palm facing down, he waved his arm as if casting a bass lure.

Abe and Tiki knew the sign. They'd seen it many times. It was the signal for them to search for enemy divers. "Be cautious."Bucky yelled, *reaffirming t*he bond of trust that raced through his heart - the cornerstone of his enduring partnership with his seafaring compatriots.

As he watched his dolphin teammates depart on their search and tag mission, the memories of the events that brought him to this place and time raced through his head.

Bucky's love for animals began when he was a kid growing up in the prominent community of Greenwich, Connecticut. His father, a Wall Street financier, had little time for his family. He was up by five, took the train to the city and seldom returned home before ten.

Likewise, his mother spent most of her day at the beauty salon, having a two martini lunch with her aristocratic gossip league or shopping at upscale boutiques leaving young Buckingham Daniels alone in a stone cold mansion.

If it wasn't for his competitive wrestling and beloved retriever, Clinger, he would have gone over to the wild side. But Clinger was always there, patiently waiting at the front door when Bucky came home from his late afternoon workout. Then, before tackling his homework, Clinger and Bucky would play ball in the spacious backyard or explore secret passages through the nearby woods.

For years they were inseparable - until one day Bucky came home from a wrestling tournament to find Clinger's lifeless body curled up on the foyer floor by the front door where he had always waited for the return of his master.

Devastated by the loss of his best friend and disillusioned by the grandiloquent haughtiness of his home environment, he joined the Navy, completed BUD/S (Basic Underwater Demolition/SEAL) training and volunteered to join the Marine Mammal Training Center in Kaneohe, Hawaii.

All SEAL dolphin handlers began training their cadets by making friends and building rapport with the members of their dolphin team. Bucky *embraced the principles of positive reinforcement and believed it was the* most effective means of influencing dolphin behavior. He soon developed a deep passion for his work with these magnanimous mammals. *Over time, his fearless dolphin teammates learned how to interpret his hand and arm signals and executed their behaviors flawlessly.*

While Bucky's hand and arm signals were widely recognized by all the dolphins under his tutelage, different trainers assigned to the program used slightly different and often confusing, signals. This required both the dolphins and new trainers to spend considerable time and effort to learn each other's idiosyncrasies.

****

Using their high-frequency sonar, Abe and Tiki swam through the ground swells of Da Nang bay searching for enemy sapper divers. Pulses of energy radiated from their melons as they scanned the water column for the echoes of unwanted intruders.

These were very special marine mammals - Alpha Team bottlenose dolphins - trained and meticulously nurtured to the highest standards. Their SEAL handlers were highly motivated operators with dolphin Vet-Tech certification. The primary mission of the dolphin teams was to provide security for US combat ships, pier facilities and storage tanks containing millions of gallons of marine diesel fuel - each an attractive target for NVA sapper divers and saboteurs.

As the senior petty officer for the CIA-sponsored Dolphin Studies Group, Chief Bucky Daniel's was on his first deployment to Vietnam. His team of dolphins were trained to find enemy divers and mark their location by releasing an inflatable red strobe buoy. Once the enemy divers were tagged, his fellow SEALs would take care of dark and dirty side of the operation commonly referred to as "*nullification*".

Daniels spoke crisply into the radio. "Zodi-one, this is DSB-one."

Chief Eddie Hanson replied, "This is Zodi-one."

"Hanson, we've got a red buoy alert from Abe. Looks like we've got enemy divers moving towards the fuel docks. Tiki has just tagged another pair. We have two sets of intruders - about thirty-meters apart. There are no bubbles. They're probably using Russian closed-circuit rigs. Di-di to our location on the double."

"We're on our way," shouted Hanson. Turning to the SEAL divers he shouted. "Buckle-up! We're heading for a sapper grab!"

"We're ready Chief," replied diver Crisp nodding to his dive buddy Walters.

"Where are the bastards?" Hanson asked as he pulled the Zodi alongside the DSB.

"Fifty yards, dead ahead. Abe and Tiki are following them. Remember the rules of engagement - the enemy must make the first offensive move," replied Bucky.

"That's bull shit," Hanson spat.

"I know. As dumb as it may be, those are the rules."

****

Enemy sappers Wang and Thieu were within six-hundred meters of their target when Wang turned to look back and immediately realized he and his dive partner were being followed by a pair of large dolphins. He released the safety on his spear gun but remained focused on his mission.

Hanson maneuvered the Zodi until it was a few meters behind Abe's bubbles.

"Crisp and Walters. I've got bubbles ten yards out. Go get 'em!" ordered Hansen.

With their masks pressed firmly against their faces, the SEAL divers fell back into the water and set a compass course towards the enemy. Using stealth techniques drilled into them during years of training and with perfectly timed precision, they reached their targets without being noticed.

Going one on one, the SEALs grasped the enemy divers from behind and severed their oxygen supply hose while maintaining a tight grip on the backside of the enemy re-breather harnesses.

Desperate to fulfill their mission, Wang and Thieu twisted and thrashed trying to escape from certain capture. Instinctively, Wang pulled the trigger of his spear gun but the shaft flew willy-nilly into the darkness.

The enemy divers continued to squirm and flail, but Crisp and Walters had perfected this capture maneuver which was virtually inescapable. Deprived of oxygen, the invading NVA divers began to feel the debilitating effects of anoxia and they passed out.

Crisp and Walters broke the surface with the unconscious sappers in tow.

"Chief, help us get these assholes aboard the Zodi!" Crisp shouted. "Cuff them and check for suicide grenades or cyanide capsules. They may not be dead."

"Hanson, this is Bucky. We've got the location of the second pair of sappers - dead ahead, about twenty yards. Let's get another pair of divers on them."

"Davis and Bridges. Bucky has another target - dead ahead - twenty yards. You should be able to intercept them from the rear and above," yelled Hanson.

While Tiki surfaced for a breath of air, Abe approached the second set of enemy divers from the rear. Sensing danger, one diver suddenly turned and caught sight of Abe. NVA suicide divers had been trained to defend themselves against American patrol dolphins and were prepared to engage these heavyweight cetaceans if necessary. The trailing NVA diver pointed his spear gun and pulled the trigger. Abe saw the incoming shaft and dipped his head to avoid a life-threatening injury. The stainless steel shaft skipped across his slippery back, piercing his muscular tail. Wounded, Abe headed for the surface squealing in pain.

"Oh, shit! Abe's hit!" bellowed Bucky. "There's a spear in his fluke. He's trying to reach us. He needs our help. Faris, you and Copeland get him back aboard the DSB. I'm re-calling Tiki.

We gotta put a major hurt on these NVA bastards!" Bucky was determined to get some payback.

Meanwhile, Davis and Bridges prepared to engage the second pair of sappers. Davis approached from above while Bridges attacked from the rear.

The enemy divers were no match for the SEALs. Their Russian oxygen re-breathers were cumbersome and not designed for speed. Increased activity overloaded their carbon dioxide absorbent system depriving them of oxygen.

Davis swam ahead, his K-bar in his right hand. As he was about to grab the invader from behind, the NVA diver turned and fired his spear gun. The triangle tip pierced Davis's wet suit, slicing through his rib cage and left ventricle.

Davis clutched the base of the spear with both hands, shocked and unable to comprehend what had happened - a stream of blood swirled into the sea. His heartbeat leaped erratically while his lungs slowly filled with salt water. Flashes of his mother's face and childhood waltzed across his mind like a super-sonic slide show. As he expelled a final stream of bubbles his eyes looked upwards and his body went limp.

Capture no longer in doubt, both NVA divers reached for their suicide grenade. Giving each other a baleful glance, they pressed their grenades to their chest and pulled the pins. With a pressure front equivalent to ten-tons, the bodies of the two NVA attackers disintegrated in a gaseous cloud of blood, tissue, organs and broken bones.

Bridges was too close to avoid injury. The shock wave ruptured both of his eardrums and damaged his spleen. Unconscious, he curled into a fetal position and drifted to the seabed.

"Fuck! We have an explosion - maybe suicide grenades. Crisp, you and Walters see what's going on," ordered Hanson.

Crisp and Walters dropped through the cloud of sand, blood and NVA body parts. Walters grabbed Bridges by his inflatable life vest and swam to the surface. Crisp found Davis and towed his body to the DSB.

"Get Bridges aboard! He needs medical attention fast! Call the hospital and have an ambulance waiting at the pier. In the meantime get his gear off and start him on oxygen!" Walters yelled.

"Fuckin suicide grenades! " Anguish was etched on Bucky's face. "Davis is dead - took a spear to the chest. Bridges might not make it. Christ, what a cluster fuck. We lost a good man and Abe has a nasty hole in his tail fluke. Damn, these fucking rules of engagement. I'm tired of watching my brothers die because of these dumb-ass rules. This is unacceptable. They give us underwater weapons and gas-darts for our dolphins but they won't let us use them unless it's a matter of life or death and the enemy shoots first! What the hell kind of rule is that? "

"What can you do?" Hanson threw up his hands.

"I'm gonna send a strong message to the CO. Hopefully he will agree and pass the message up the chain of command. We can't screw around like this. Shit, this is war - not a pussy-footin' square dance. We should dispatch enemy invaders on sight - without warning. Fuck these suicide sappers - they're enemy combatants. They're trained to kill us without hesitation. Our dolphins need to use lethal force - a gas dart to the chest and they could have nullified them in seconds. Those fuckers wouldn't even see it coming. And Davis would still be alive."

NO LIFEGUARD ON DUTY
Legacy of a Navy SEAL

Synopsis

In the wild ocean, there is no lifeguard on duty.

He thought his only love would be the ocean - until he met Lynn and he found himself fighting a battle to balance his career as a SEAL and the woman he loved. He left the SEALs to become a pioneer in the deep sea diving industry. Trapped between the call of the sea and his family, he struggled to find a harmonious balance between the woman he loved and seductive globetrotting adventures.

HELL WEEK

Hell Week, the fourth week of training, was designed to identify men who would rather endure the pain or even die - than quit. We were promised Hell Week would be a massive, twenty-four hour a day adrenaline rush - emotionally packed with fear and pain. Men who would rather be doing something else were offered many opportunities to do so. BUD/S instructors tempted and taunted every tadpole - promising a hot shower - a warm bunk and all the sleep they wanted. But they had to quit.

The party started Sunday night. It was a few minutes after ten when the instructors tossed yellow smoke and flash-bang grenades inside our barracks.

"Get dressed in greens and fall out on the street facing the bay. You have three minutes!" shouted an instructor over a portable loudspeaker.

Coughing and gagging - we rushed to comply with the order and soon found ourselves standing in the middle of the street nervously awaiting our fate.

"Attention!" shouted Chief Price. "Right- face! Forward - march!"

We marched down the wooden pier towards the moonlit bay.

"Company - halt! Right - face!"

There was a ten-foot drop to the cold ocean.

"Forward - march!"

We marched off the pier into San Diego Bay.

"Is this all they got?" said one of my classmates.

Doc Barber, our class corpsman, heard the comment and responded accordingly.

"What's so fucking funny?" His left cheek was filled with a golf-ball size hunk of chewing tobacco. "You lads need to take this a bit more seriously. Muster up on the street. We're going to repeat this until you get it right. And wipe those shitty smiles off your face. I can assure you, gentlemen - you ain't seen nothing yet - and it ain't gonna be funny."

Instructors were always watching and waiting for any mistake. As each of man exited the bay he was ordered to do twenty push-ups and jump back into the water. This harassment continued until midnight. Some trainees were ordered to climb into a large diving bell where they were subjected to a blast of high-pressure water from a fire hose.

Again, we were ordered to put on dry greens and muster up on the street. As it turned out, this was a repeat performance of the first dunkings. The objective of this evolution was to get every item of clothing we possessed, jerseys, trousers, underwear, socks, and boots, soaking wet. This is how it was to be for the rest of Hell Week, wet and cold.

Each man burned five to six thousand calories per day. The extra calories were needed to replace what we burned and to offset sleep deprivation. When it was time for one of our four meals per day, we had to run, often a mile or more, to the chow hall, with a rubber boat bouncing atop our heads.

"Down, boats," came the order. "You have 30-minutes to eat, take a dump and prepare for the next evolution."

"Hooyah!"

I wolfed down my meal in a matter of minutes and had extra time to visit head or take a brief catnap. Amazingly, I managed to quickly fall asleep sitting on the concrete. Fifteen minutes of sleep, four times a day provided an extra hour of refuge in an otherwise endless day. During the first three days of Hell Week, except for my brief mealtime snoozes, none of us received any sleep.

I had never seen a Navy SEAL in person until I reported to BUD/S. Olivera was the first. The SEAL Teams had been commissioned eight months earlier - with the original fifty plank owners of SEAL Team One coming from the ranks of the Underwater Demolition Teams 11 and 12.

"Listen up. You're going to meet some of the men from SEAL Team One," said Chief Price with a tone of respect. "These men are here to make sure you have what it takes to become a frogman and to keep you occupied 24-hours a day. Those who graduate may someday have the opportunity to join them."

During the first two days of Hell Week, about two dozen tadpoles gave up their quest. Maybe it was the cold water, log-PT or sleep deprivation. In many cases, it was a combination of factors. One by one, the quitters quietly walked up to an instructor and whispered, "I quit. I've had enough."

The mud flats were a stinky, nasty experience. This decaying black pool of slime was located about eight miles from our base at the south end of the bay. It was part mud, tidal crud and storm run-off with the stench of rotten eggs.

Here, squirming, worm-like critters made their home. These two-inch long invertebrates slithered in and out of our clothing, up our legs and arms. They sometimes wiggled their way inside our jersey's and trousers. Lucky for us, these slimy creatures didn't bite or attach their mouth parts to our unprotected skin. Nevertheless, like leeches, they provided an extra measure of anxiety and in some cases, outright panic.

Each boat crew carried their boat on their heads the eight miles from the base to the mud flats. When we arrived, we were ordered to place a couple of boats upside down at the very edge of the muck. These were used as a trampoline for the diving competition.

Each tadpole was ordered to perform a fancy, headfirst dive into the putrid goop. Those that didn't become completely covered in the muck on their first dive were punished with twenty push-ups and another attempt to impress the instructors. Our day was filled with relay races, back flips, wrestling matches and caterpillar swims designed to keep us covered in a thick layer of muck. Several men quit before lunch.

At noon, those remaining were instructed to sit in a circle - up to our necks in the slurry. We were each given a cold chicken breast, a chocolate chip cookie, an apple and a small carton of milk, neatly packaged in a white cardboard box.

"Hooyah, we finally get to eat," someone shouted.

"But wait! We're covered head to toe in stinking mud," another complained.

"What the hell are you complaining about? You're not having lunch at the Hotel Del. This is all you get. I don't give a damn if you eat it or not," one of the instructors barked.

There were no means to clean the muck from our hands, fingers, mouths or faces and the instructors certainly didn't care.

The first round of explosives detonated shortly after everyone began to eat their meal. Hundreds of pounds of south bay slime erupted from our perimeter, coating our unprotected meals with viscous mud. Several tadpoles quit during the afternoon mud flat session.

****

The San Diego Bay boat paddle commenced at sunset on Thursday night. It was planned as an all night evolution with the leading boat scheduled to finish by six o'clock Friday morning. Boats completing the paddle before six in the morning were awarded an hour of sleep.

Each boat was required to paddle to the south end of the bay and back, a distance of thirty-two miles as the cormorant flies.

However, everyone now suffered from sleep deprivation making simple navigation problems a dicey game of speculation.

Accurate navigation was not the only challenge. Sleep deprivation caused many tadpoles to experience some level of psychedelic impairment and vivid hallucinations.

Sometime after midnight, midway to our destination, my crewmate, Albie Matherne, suddenly let out a loud scream and began swinging his paddle wildly in the air.

"It's a flying dragon! He's trying to get me! I'm getting outta here!" Albie shouted in his altered state and promptly jumped into the bay. The cold water quickly brought him back to reality and he clamored back into the boat.

"Let's keep it all together. Focus on our objective. See those lights up ahead. That's where we are going!" yelled our skipper.

Some boat crews paddled in circles. Others stopped at beachside party campfires only to be caught by the instructors and punished for their transgression. Hell Week was designed to simulate actual combat conditions where sleep is often not an option.

This was also a critical evaluation process for the officers. They were responsible for navigating the route, keeping their crew aware of their progress and demonstrating effective leadership skills.

Early Friday evening the remaining boat crews formed up on the beach to compete in a twelve-hour treasure hunt over a 20-mile land and sea route. This evolution combined surf passage, ocean and bay paddles, plus miles of trekking up and down the Silver Strand beach while carrying our boat atop our heads. Each crew was given a clue to their next checkpoint. If they missed it, the crew suffered a penalty and were ordered to return to their last checkpoint before continuing. This was our final evolution before securing from Hell Week. We placed second and for this achievement, we were rewarded with two hours of sleep.

On Saturday morning, we were ordered to the football field for a final evolution and debriefing. Chief Allen led us in a series of physical training exercises, followed by a four mile run around the track.

At noon, Chief Price approached.

"Congratulations gentlemen. Hell Week is now secured. You have the rest of the weekend to sleep and heal. We will commence week five at 0700 Monday."

The goal of separating the men from the others was accomplished. Over three dozen wanna-be's had quit or been dropped in the previous week.

Our boat skipper stood up and explored the face of each member of his crew. "Congratulations men. We all made it. I'm very proud of your efforts. We are the only boat to finish the first four weeks with the original crew."

The officers and men of Class 29 mingled about congratulating and backslapping each other before walking off to our sleeping quarters. Some men went straight to bed - flopped down on their bunk without even taking off their clothes. Others took a hot shower and then hit the sack.

Sunday was a day to relax and contemplate what we had achieved. There were sixty-three enlisted men and seven officers remaining. I was proud to be one of them. No longer was my cup half-empty - rather, it was now half-full.

Tadpole at the mud flats

About the Author

Craig is a former Navy SEAL, Vietnam vet and a pioneer in the deep-sea diving industry. His underwater adventures have taken him to the deepest and most hostile parts of the North Sea, South East Asia, Australia, New Zealand, and South America. He's worked with bottlenose dolphins, undersea habitats, submersibles, remote controlled underwater vehicles and experimental diving equipment. .

He lives in Southern California with his wife, Lynn.

Made in the USA
San Bernardino, CA
06 March 2018